THE CAPER
OF THE
GOLDEN BULLS

Other Books by William P. McGivern

A CHOICE OF ASSASSINS

A PRIDE OF PLACE

POLICE SPECIAL, *Comprising Three Complete Novels:*
  The Seven File
  The Darkest Hour
  Rogue Cop

THE ROAD TO THE SNAIL

SEVEN LIES SOUTH

SAVAGE STREETS

ODDS AGAINST TOMORROW

NIGHT EXTRA

THE SEVEN FILE

THE DARKEST HOUR

ROGUE COP

MARGIN OF TERROR

THE BIG HEAT

THE CROOKED FRAME

SHIELD FOR MURDER

VERY COLD FOR MAY

HEAVEN RAN LAST

BUT DEATH RUNS FASTER

With Maureen Daly McGivern

MENTION MY NAME IN MOMBASA

THE CAPER
OF THE
GOLDEN BULLS

By William P. McGivern

Dodd, Mead & Company
New York

Library of Congress Catalog Card Number: 66-13479

Printed in the United States of America
by Vail-Ballou Press, Inc., Binghamton, N. Y.

To Ferdinand Zogbaum III
who ran so truly and well
that year

THE CAPER
OF THE
GOLDEN BULLS

1 ᔈ

ON PLEASANT MORNINGS Peter Churchman enjoyed swimming in the *piscina* at the foot of his garden. It was a charming little pool, enclosed by oleanders and a bathhouse crimson with bougainvillea, but it had been constructed, oddly enough, without a drain; when it was necessary to change the water, Peter's maids, and some of their friends from nearby villas, kicked off their *alpargatas,* put on old uniforms, jumped into the pool, and emptied it with buckets.

It was tedious work, but the girls made a holiday of it, splashing about the pool as busily as wrens in a bird bath; and when they were finished they scrubbed the sides and bottom clean with coarse tufts of *esparto* grass which they twisted from the slopes of the mountain behind the villa.

After all this it took the pool three days to fill. Once

1

upon a time Peter had found this mildly annoying, but that was before his conversion to the philosophical view; after that significant event he had come easily and naturally to the conclusion that a temporarily inoperative swimming pool was a light cross indeed to carry through life.

Most men acquire the philosophical view with a deliberate intellectual effort, or because they have no other choice. Not so with Peter. One morning he had waked with the thought—brilliant and final as a lightning bolt—that he had wasted far too much time worrying about things that were never going to happen to him.

All his life—all his adult life, at any rate—Peter had dreaded only three things: going to prison; losing his hair; losing his keen physical interest in women. Now it seemed fairly obvious that he had escaped—and would continue to escape—these inhibiting disasters. He had come through—that was his phrase for it. He had come through the battle intact.

Of prison, there was no longer any threat at all. And not only had he kept his hair, but it remained black as pitch, except for the silver wings at his temples, and these Peter rather liked. And of the last dread worry, he could snap his fingers at that too, for he was at the moment more ardently and heartily in love than ever before in his life.

With the realization that he had come through, Peter

relaxed, and life became an undiluted joy. He knew that he had not got a big truth by the tail. To understand that one's fears are groundless may be comforting; but to act on that information was exhilarating. It was a little truth, a little knowledge, but it brought great peace to Peter Churchman.

Rather self-consciously, he began to keep a journal. The first entry read simply: *If a man has no goals in life, he can usually find good roads to travel.*

Peter was not sure that this was philosophy. But he understood what it meant in relation to himself, and that was what mattered. As the happy peaceful days went by, he began searching for more glitterings of truth. When he found one he brought it back to his journal like a magpie. He never discovered a great diamond of truth, only the ones that were like bits and pieces of colored glass. But these served their purpose, and in time they provided him many rosy windows from which to look out upon the world. They gave him a picture of things which coincided quite marvelously with his new philosophy.

They enabled him, for instance, to consider with tolerance, if not relish, his astonishing conversation with Grace at dinner the previous night.

At the memory of it Peter dove into the pool without removing his bathrobe.

She had said: "I know you hate surprises. But I must tell you. I have three children."

Sensibly Peter had put down his fork; otherwise he might have put it in his eye.

"Why in God's name didn't you tell me before?"

"While you were making up your mind about me, it didn't seem fair. To the children, that is."

"But how about me! Did you think about being fair to me?"

"Oh, Peter. They're such dears."

"Now please listen and please try to understand. I don't like children. It's not because I'm selfish or insensitive. It's just a glandular reaction. It's the same way I feel about sauerkraut or Martinis."

"That's very strange."

"Come on. Lots of people don't like children."

"No, I meant about the sauerkraut. Did you ever try it with carroway seeds?"

"Grace! This is serious. Why did you decide to tell me now? On this particular night?"

"Well, my hand was forced, so to speak. My husband wants me to come back to him. That's why I went to Paris last month."

"Oh, does he! Tired of his garret and his silly paintings and prostitutes. Now he wants to get back to the fireside, back to all your blue chips."

She had shaken her finger at him, a tiny gesture of admonition; even in his agitation he had found it endearing.

"No. Guy is very rich. But he has principles. That's

4

why he wouldn't give me alimony."

"He's a principled tightwad, I'd say."

"You don't understand. He feels alimony is demeaning. He doesn't think a woman should be financially penalized for remarrying. He gave me a million dollars when I left him."

"Oh. Where are your children?"

"They just arrived this morning. They were in Venice with my mother."

"I didn't even know you had a mother."

"You might have presumed that much."

"Now please, Grace." After a long moment he had said: "Darling, let's not spoil things. Your children, your little dears, do they, well, chatter a lot?"

She had smiled radiantly, "Oh, I do love you, Peter."

Shaken and dispirited, Peter had gone home to write in his journal: *She is tall as a silver beech tree. Bonfires of excitement blaze in her eyes. She is an orchestra of sex. Throbbing drums sounding the charge. Pinwheels of excitement flashing in the tympani. Bugles and trumpets screaming splendid abandonment. Violas (contra-bassoons?) sobbing the final surrender. But she has three children!* After a moment of thought, Peter had written: *Boarding school?* He had underlined this three times, with mounting excitement, and had gone to bed in a fairly cheerful frame of mind.

Peter pulled himself from the pool and removed his dripping bathrobe. The sun climbed in a white sky.

5

Fresh warm breezes from the sea stirred the flowers and the air became soft and fragrant. You've come through, he reminded himself. You didn't go to prison. You didn't lose your hair. And you have Grace, from drums to violas. Or contra-bassoons.

He drew a deep breath and squared his shoulders, sustained and enriched by the exhilarating conviction that the worst would never happen; he had come through the battle intact, and the years of peace stretched ahead of him as invitingly as a field of violets on a spring day.

He began his exercises. Once Peter had been rather vain about his physical strength and condition. Now his workouts were brief; stomach exercises, a hundred-odd push-ups, nothing more.

A maid called a name from the terrace, her voice soaring up in the mild air like a flute. The owner of the name came through the opening in the oleander hedge: Antonio Gonzalez y Najera, the policeman of the village, tidy, stout, cheerful.

He said: "Peter, you're under arrest."

Peter collapsed in the middle of a push-up, clutched at his hair.

"I'm sorry, Peter. I'm joking, of course." Antonio looked at him severely. "But I have a parking summons for you. Yesterday you left your car in front of the burros' drinking fountain."

"But just for a few minutes."

6

"I'm sorry. It was closer to an hour." Antonio sat on a bamboo stool, removed his cap, and fanned his face. "You must set a good example for the tourists. You are a permanent resident, a businessman with a bar and restaurant, a man of substance and property." He sighed. "Tourists. I live in a village of strangers. Sometimes through the glitter of sports shirts and cameras I see a familiar face. An old man I went to school with. A widow with white hair whom I chased squealing through the olive trees in my youth. They are like ghosts." He sighed again. "Everything is changing. They are sending our Virgin to Pamplona for the fiesta of San Fermin. Did you know that?"

"No."

"She has never left the village before. But everything is changing today. The fact that a thing exists condemns it. It must be changed. Regardless of the expense."

"How's that?"

"It's just been announced. All the Virgins—from Seville, Malaga, Granada, Cordova, from all the cities—are being sent to Pamplona." He sighed deeply. "One will be named Queen of San Fermin."

"Like a beauty contest?"

"I think a more tasteful name might be found for it."

"I'm sorry," Peter said.

"Of course. But the expense. To crate the Virgin, to insure her jewels, poor as they are, to transport her to

Pamplona, to make certain she is securely guarded. It's an enormous expense."

"I don't have a checkbook here at the pool, Antonio."

Antonio looked at him in surprise. "Why do you want a checkbook?"

"Well, I'm practically a native son. I'd like to help out. Make a contribution to the Virgin's trip."

"It's not necessary."

"I'd like to, Antonio."

"Then I imagine it can be arranged. I'll stop by later at the bar." He looked through his pockets. "I can't find your summons, Peter. I may have lost it. If I find it, I'll put it in the mail."

He went away and the maids called Peter to his breakfast.

In shorts and sandals he drank American coffee and ate Danish bacon, items sent to him regularly by Mr. Shahari, the Indian money changer in Gibraltar. The maids chattered around him in high, cheerful voices; of the evils of the egg woman; the perfidies of the bread man, the wood man, the gypsy beggars. They were the epic poets of the village, writing on air the high drama of the drunken fisherman, the burned child, the fifty-peseta note blown from the window sill and lost forever in the sands.

Grace came onto the terrace through the living room doors. In a white dress and golden sandals she drew all the color from the flowers, all the light from the sky; to

8

Peter she seemed the glittering center of the universe.

"Darling, I've brought you a little surprise. Debby, say hello to Mr. Churchman."

The child at her side said, "Hello, Mr. Churchman."

"Now what a pleasant surprise!" Peter said rather too heartily. "How old are you, Debby?"

"I'm eight."

"Still in grade school I expect."

"Yes."

"Would you like some cookies? A glass of milk?"

"She's had a huge breakfast, Peter. Debby, be a good child. Go off and find something to play with. I'm sure there are cats."

The child went away and Grace sat down opposite Peter. She looked at him with splendid loving eyes and said, "I don't think it's violas *or* contra-bassoons. Cellos maybe?"

"Grace! You've been in my journal."

"It was on the table in the hall. Like a guest book. I looked at a page, which began, 'She is tall as a silver beech tree' so I knew it was about me. It was lovely, Peter. Bonfires of excitement. Bugles and trumpets. But it made me very sad."

"Why?"

"I have another surprise for you, I'm afraid. I'm pregnant."

The child came onto the terrace and said: "Mommy, I found a cat."

9

"How nice, dear."

"It made a mess on the floor."

"Well, tell the maid, dear."

"How? I can't speak Spanish."

"Tell her *el gatto aguaed* on the floor."

"I don't think he *aguaed*."

"Dear. Well, just tell the maid. She'll cope."

The child went back into the living room. Peter took Grace's hand in his, and smiled at her indulgently.

"You can't be pregnant, darling. I'm sure of it. Trust me."

She withdrew her hands. "It's not you, for heaven's sake. It's my husband. Guy."

"How fortunate he wants you back."

"Oh, how cruel you are. I see what satisfaction this gives you!"

"Now, Grace! Don't try to put me on the defensive."

"How could I do that? Unless it's where you belong!"

From the living room they heard shrill and righteous exclamations from a maid; the defiant snarl of the cat; the swipe of a broom; the slam of a door; the sloshing of water on the floor.

"It was last month, when I went up to Paris. I hardly knew you then, Peter."

"I see."

"In France, we are still technically man and wife. It's some legal, religious arrangement with Mexico."

"How interesting."

10

She sighed. "I was prepared for anything. Anything but provincial sniffs. Well. I see you've made up your mind about me."

They went into the long, somberly furnished living room, dark and cool after the sunny terrace.

"Come on, Debby. We've got to be going."

The child lay on her stomach looking at an American magazine. She was really quite small, Peter thought; slim white arms and legs, neck no thicker than a banana.

"How much does she weigh?"

"What an odd question! Were you thinking of roasting her or something?"

"Well, no. Is she the oldest?"

"Yes. Why?"

Face the violet fields of peace gratefully, Peter told himself; remember you came through the battle intact.

"Well, if you packed them all together—figuratively speaking, I mean—they'd hardly displace one normal-size adult."

"Pack them? In what? A trunk?"

"Don't be idiotic. I know they're distinct individuals. With private paths to travel, with immortal souls to save, with dreams as distinct as their fingerprints." He wondered fleetingly if he believed this, decided it didn't matter, pressed on. "I'm not a brute. But, Grace, in a physical sense, in a manageable sense, they're more like *one* person than three. Bulkwise that is."

"You're just playing around with words. To make it all right."

"Well, of course."

She looked at him tremulously, meltingly, and touched his cheek with the back of her fingers. "Do you wonder that I love you?"

"Mushy stuff," the child said frowning.

Peter thought of boarding schools in northern climes. Train stations shuttered up, airfields socked in, Christmas carols sounding in drafty dormitories. Great educational freezers full of trapped children. Cheery wires to snowbound kiddies: Chins up, see you in the spring.

Grace said, "Peter, what are you grinning at?"

"Just at how wonderful it's going to be."

"Mushy stuff."

"True, true," he said, smiling at the child.

At Peter's bar in the central plaza of the village, an American girl named Cathy Clark pleaded with Mario for a drink. She was nineteen, intense and nervous, with a slim figure, curly brown hair, neat wrists and ankles, and a surprisingly pleasant voice. When Peter arrived she sighed with relief and took her appeal to this higher court.

"Peter, please explain to Mario I'm not *drunk*. I'm heartbroken, demoralized, shattered, but I'm not *drunk*."

"Maybe a nap is what you need."

"I'm not sleepy. I couldn't sleep. And I don't really

want a drink. I just want to talk to someone."

"Okay, come in my office."

Peter glanced at his mail while Cathy told him about someone named Morgan. From his desk he had a view of the barroom and the terrace facing the plaza. The tables were filling up with bearded young Americans, families of French people, Britishers taking a whiskey or sherry before setting out to tramp about the mountains.

"He pushed me down the stairs, and said I shouldn't be allowed to have children. He said I should be innoculated, so I couldn't contaminate people with my selfishness."

Peter picked up an envelope and glanced casually at the handwriting. The letters swam abruptly before his eyes; he felt shock going through his body in steady, rhythmic beats; a cold knot of tension gathering painfully in his stomach.

"Dear God," he said.

"Yes. And he told me that if I had a soul it would have dollar signs on it."

The envelope bore the name and crest of the Pez Espada, a smart hotel a few miles down the coast. Peter's name, in dreadfully familiar, back-slanted handwriting, gleamed in purple ink (also dreadfully familiar) on the snowy face of the envelope, which bore no stamp. Peter ripped open the envelope, pulled out a single sheet of paper. There was his name again; a room

13

number, 401, and another name, also dreadfully familiar —Angela—written in a flourish which terminated in a pair of mocking exclamation points.

"No!" he said, and put a hand to his racing heart.

"It's true, Peter. Every word of it."

"Get out of here."

"What?" The word was a startled bleat.

"Get out of here. Wash your face. Get some sleep, you silly child. Stop dumping the dustbins of your psyche in my office. Out."

She glowed under the rebuke; she believed that men masked passion with exasperation and boredom. "Yes, Peter," she said gratefully. "I understand." And crept from his office.

Peter closed the door and dialed the Pez Espada. "Pepe, this is Peter Churchman. I need some information. Who is in room four-o-one?"

"One moment. I'll see. Ah. Yes. Monsieur and Madame Francois Morel."

"What's she like?"

"Pale, dark-haired, petite. Once she must have been very pretty. Like a kitten."

Christ, he thought; there was no mistake; it was Angela.

"And her husband?"

"Handsome, slender, carries himself well. He seems used to good things."

A flicker of hope warmed Peter's breast. Perhaps she

14

had landed a fat one. Perhaps his alarm was premature; she might want nothing but a drink, a toast to the old days. But Pepe's next words doused this feeble flame like a jet of ice water.

"But he's not used to paying for them, I think."

"Listen carefully. They may ask you if I called. Say no. If they offer you money, I'll go one thousand pesetas over their best offer. Okay?"

"That's not necessary, Senor Churchman."

"I don't want our friendship to work a hardship on you."

"If you put it in those terms, I can only accept. Thank you."

Peter left his office and hurried to the bar. Greetings sailed toward him from a half-dozen tables; invitations for elevens; for golf; for fishing. Peter's presence turned on smiles; in six years he had become a popular fixture in the life of the village.

He called Mario to the end of the bar and showed him the letter from Angela.

"Who brought this?"

"A man, a Frenchman."

"Tell me about him, Mario," Peter said, and the urgency in his tone brought a cooperative frown to Mario's plump face.

"He's tall—not as tall as you though—and slender. He walks well. He may have been an officer. He's about forty. Dark hair, quite handsome. He wore a blazer, flannel slacks. His manners are good, but I have an impression—" Mario rocked a hand judiciously—"that he acquired them by observing. Not at home. Not at school."

Peter matched Mario's description against various index cards in his mind, and drew blanks. Someone new then. Not Bendell. Not Canalli. Not the Irishman.

Wearily he said, "Please give me a double vodka, Mario."

Mario raised his eyebrows. "Is something wrong?"

"Now whatever gave you that idea?"

Peter drummed is fingers on the bar. Mario shrugged and poured him a double vodka.

2 ∿

IN A SENSE Francois Morel's eyes were the best of his features; insolent, greedy, but frankly so; the rest might have been made in a factory. When he put on sunglasses to join the woman sunning herself on the terrace of their suite, his face became a brownly neutral oblong, devoid of weakness, strength, or character of any kind at all.

"You talked to the desk clerk?" asked Angela, without opening her eyes. She wore a bikini and shimmering layers of sun lotion.

"Twice. He says he doesn't even know Peter Churchman."

"Did you offer him money?"

"Of course." Francois sat on the lounge beside Angela. "You said Peter Churchman would come flying to your side. So?"

17

"So! Most men would. But he's not like most men."

She turned onto her back. Under a cap of metallic black hair, Angela's features were unpleasantly hard and sharp, but, at thirty-five, her body was still tiny and exquisite; when she twisted to a more comfortable position, the movements hollowed out a shining concavity between her ribs and her loins, and caused the muscles in her thighs to tremble like silken cords being gently agitated beneath a satin coverlet.

This excellence was a memorial, in a sense, to an esthetic father who had worshipped her doll-like fragility, and had imbedded in her unconscious the compulsions to preserve it. But none of his gentle injunctions and rebukes and denials had been able to preserve her face. Once it had been as smooth and pretty as the surface of a pond fed by healthy springs; but then, it seemed, the springs had dried up and the water had become streaked and marred by things from the depths that were forcing themselves to the surface.

This was an irony she had lost the capacity to savor. For many years Angela had been amused by the contrast between certain of her needs, and the shell-like forehead and discreetly masked eyes which hid them from the world. But she was no longer amused by this, for the thing inside her was no longer concealed from view; each year it became more obvious, more recognizable, boldly peering from eyes, lurking insolently at the corners of her mouth. One day the bitch thing would claw through to the surface, to mock at the world it hated through *her* eyes, to deride it with her *lips*.

Life would not be pleasant for the old witch she would eventually turn into, Angela knew; it would, in fact, be sheer, bloody hell, unless she were financially secure. She could not, as a result of her father's training, ask favors of people; to beg or wheedle caused pains in her head and stomach that were beyond enduring. For several years now the only thing that could brighten her eye or excite her senses was the prospect of money.

Francois took her hand, squeezed it gently. "We need Peter Churchman, my dear."

She opened her eyes and studied him gravely. "You're overdressed."

"Am I?"

"Yes. You've dyed your hair. Lost thirty pounds. Put lifts in your shoes. But you still hang yourself like a Christmas tree."

Francois removed his glasses and studied what he was wearing, puzzled: brown suede shoes, light flannel slacks, a blue blazer, snowy white shirt, a blue cravat; wrist watch, a silver ID bracelet, an opal ring.

"I think I'm dressed quite well."

"You are not."

"Don't be unpleasant, darling."

"I'm being instructive."

"It's the same thing really."

19

Angela sighed. "All right. Peter will come here, don't worry. I want you to remember something. He can fool you with his manner. He makes jokes and appears to take things lightly. He flew with the RAF before the United States came into the war. I think he enjoys playing the silly ass; it's something he must have picked up from the British. But I want you to keep this in mind: He is the most dangerous man I ever knew."

"All women say that about their ex-lovers. It gives dead affairs significance."

"I'd hardly say that about you, Francois."

"I'm not dangerous?"

"No."

"Please don't be unpleasant again, dear. Or instructive."

"You're only dangerous because you're without any concept of loyalty."

He was still holding her hand. Smiling, he bent it slowly down toward the fleshy part of her forearm. She turned her head aside and closed her eyes. The tendons in her throat stood out.

"Well?"

She was silent.

"Well?"

The ugly conflict lasted no more than a minute.

"Stop it," she said quietly.

"And?"

"Please." The word sounded small and cramped, as if

it had been squeezed out of shape by the straining cords in her throat.

"Of course. I don't like being childish, darling. But instruction exasperates me."

She let out her breath slowly, but didn't open her eyes.

"All right, forget the instructions. Forget everything, Francois, except that our lives depend on Peter Churchman. And that he is dangerous. We are going to make him do something that he will not want to do. We'll have a tiger on our leash, not a tabby cat."

He smiled. "I commanded a company in Algeria. One man is very much like another, I discovered; their breaking points are simply in different places."

The phone in the suite rang. Angela hurried to answer it.

"Peter, darling!" she cried joyously. "How wonderful to hear your voice again. Do come right up."

"Angela, how delightful." Peter kissed her cheek. "How marvelous!" He kissed her other cheek, held her at arm's length, beamed at her. "You found it! You must have! That fountain Senor de Leon was hunting for." He smiled at Francois. "Ponce, of course?" Stop it, he thought, with a flutter of panic. Only fools giggle on cracking ice. "Angela, I mean it! You look wonderful. You haven't changed a bit."

"It's nice to hear, even if it isn't true. And this is Francois Morel. Francois, Peter Churchman."

"Can I get you a drink?" Francois asked him.

"Fine idea. Orange juice?"

"I'll ring down for it."

"Oh never mind. Just a glass of vodka."

"A glass?"

"Yes, old man. With one ice cube."

In the sunny, expensively cluttered suite, Peter felt as if he were walking a tightrope across a crocodile-infested gorge. The sea beyond the terrace winked with a thousand sunny lights, and fishing boats skimmed like white birds against the blue horizon. Angela and Francois looked rich and comfortable. Handsome luggage stood about everywhere. A carton of cigarettes, a tin of caviar, a mink-lined raincoat were heaped cozily in the lap of a chair. A bottle of Moet et Chandon and a pair of evening slippers with rhinestone heels stood on a portable record player.

They were on the wing! Relief flooded through him, warming the cold knot of anxiety in his stomach. Smiling widely he accepted a glass from Francois.

"Now look. Am I going to be able to give you lunch? Or dinner? I imagine you're just passing through, but still and all—"

He trailed off. Angela was watching him with an odd little smile. "No, we're staying on, Peter," she said.

"Grand," he said, and drained the glass of vodka.

They were both smiling at him, he realized; appraisingly, confidently.

"Another drink?"

"Thanks, Francois. Thanks very much."

Near the windows of the terrace stood a motion picture screen; a projector faced it from a table a dozen feet away. Somehow, their presence seemed ominous. Peter distrusted the incongruous, for he knew from experience how simple it was to trick people with unexpected juxtapositions of ideas or objects. All his antennae were quivering now, reading the winds for danger. He knew his alarm had been justified; the warm, fragrant air fairly cracked with tension.

Francois gave him a fresh drink and Angela settled herself comfortably on a lemon-colored lounge. She wore a white linen beach coat, with a blue sash at the waist. As she crossed her legs, and allowed her body to compose itself gracefully on the pillows, Peter noted that the claws of time had been greedily at work on her features. Basic Angela was showing through, no doubt of it; the cupidity and corruption that had lain in wait so long and patiently under the creamy-white flesh was becoming bolder with the years, blurring and coarsening the rosy features, whose blandness and innocence had once prompted people to exclaim at the appropriateness of her given name, Angela.

"Peter, is this something new?"

"What's that?"

"You didn't used to drink in the daytime."

"Oh. Well, just the odd sherry now and then."

"Would you prefer sherry?" Francois asked with a smile.

"No, this is fine."

Angela sighed. "Peter, this isn't going to be pleasant. So I might as well get on with it. We need your help."

"Things have been going rather well for me, as a matter of fact," Peter said, although he realized bleakly it wasn't money they wanted; he was stalling in a largely futile effort to gird himself for what was coming. "How much do you need?"

"This isn't a touch," Angela said. "You knew that, of course."

"All right. What is it?"

"We need your help to rob a bank, Peter."

"Ha, ha. Very good," he said.

"Peter dear. I wasn't trying to be funny."

That was suddenly quite obvious to Peter. He managed a smile. "I presume you mean you'd like some advice. A few pointers. Very well. In the first place, I strongly recommend that you forget it. Put it right out of your mind."

Angela smiled. Excitement glittered deep in her eyes. "We don't want advice, Peter. We want much more than that." She drew her fingernails slowly across her bare kneecap where they left marks like tiny ski-trails on the snowy flesh, and, Peter recalled, with a premonitory pang, that the only times Angela savored such perverse stimuli was when she held all the aces in the game.

He began pacing. The Frenchman smiled at Angela, who was watching Peter with the same clinical interest she might have accorded an insect struggling on a pin. "We want you to plan the job," she said, quite amiably. "We want you to tell us who and what we'll need. The timetable, the execution, will all be in your hands. And of course, Peter dear, we want you to lead us, to lead us as brilliantly and fearlessly as you did—" she began to smile with excitement—"in those days when you were known to Scotland Yard, to the Sûreté, to Interpol—but only as that shadowy menace, the Black Dove."

"Angela, you were never intelligent," Peter said. "But neither were you stupid."

"There's nothing to worry about. I've told Francois all about you."

"And I am as the grave," Francois said with a bow, a smile.

Peter looked steadily at Angela. "I didn't believe you could be this stupid. This foolish."

"I'm not foolish, Peter. I'm very serious."

"We are deadly serious," Francois said. "You can save a lot of time and trouble if you remember that."

Peter was still staring at Angela.

"Did you hear me?" asked Francois, a touch of color in his cheeks.

25

"I heard you," Peter said, without looking at him. "Now please shut up. I think, on what I admit may be insufficient evidence, that you're a tiresome person. Angela, you've done a stupid thing coming here. A phase of our lives ended ten years ago. For you and me, for Bendell, for the Irishman, for Canalli. Each of us accomplished what we set out to. And we agreed to give it up. We agreed never to meet again. To keep away from one another, to put oceans between us. We've been lucky. But the police have a substitute for luck—patience. They can wait, sipping hot coffee in their dusty offices, until someone makes a mistake. And you may have just made that mistake."

"You got what you wanted," Angela said stonily. "But I didn't."

"My God, you had millions."

"It's gone. I gambled. I made bad investments."

Peter glanced briefly at Francois. "Yes, I see."

"I don't mind your being unpleasant," Francois said. "It may be the other way round soon. Let me remind you again, we are deadly serious."

"And so am I. Let me repeat: My answer is no."

Francois looked surprised. "You don't want to know the details? The amount of money involved?"

"I most certainly do not. Angela, I won't insist on squatters' rights to Spain. Since you are here, I shall leave. That will reduce the danger to both of us. I shall come back in a month or so. In my absence, I trust you

26

will do the decent thing and go elsewhere. Far elsewhere."

He gave them unsmiling nods and turned resolutely toward the door. As his hand touched the knob, he heard what he knew he would hear, Angela's voice: "Peter dear, don't go just yet. I want to show you something."

Of course, he thought hopelessly, she would be holding aces.

"I'm rather rushed for time."

"This won't take long. Francois, draw the curtains."

The room became dim. Peter squared his shoulders: The darkness seemed to him a symbolic blindfold, the initial formality accompanying his execution.

"Would you like to sit beside me, Peter?"

"I'm quite comfortable, thank you."

"You once liked to stroke my ankles. Remember? It amused you that you could circle them with your thumb and forefinger." In the gloom her teeth flashed in a smile. "And you said once that my body must have been created by magicians and glassblowers."

"A pretty speech," Francois said judiciously.

Peter stood mute, thinking black thoughts. He had come through, but only to *this:* to be baited by jackals.

Francois turned on the projector and the screen flickered to life.

The scene that came imperfectly to view was vaguely familiar to Peter: a wide and busy avenue in a large city; pedestrians hurrying along sidewalks; policemen at intersections stopping and starting thick sluggish lanes of traffic; a slanting rain falling over everything.

Francois made an adjustment; the images became sharper.

"Now that's much better," Angela said. "I was sure my films weren't so poor. Do you remember this, Peter?"

"Indeed I do." He smiled faintly. "Lisbon, isn't it?"

"Of course."

They looked at a large and formidable building, with barred doors and massive intricacies of ironwork guarding its windows. Near the doors, set into the stone walls, was a sturdy bronze plaque; the letters on its surface were obscured by the fuming rain.

"Can you read what it says, Peter?"

"I don't need to." He experienced a pang of nostalgia, as he recalled the challenge of this fortress; the problems it had presented; the risks it had involved; and the rewards it had given them in the end. "September, 1958, wasn't it? The Banco Commerciale?"

"But of course."

"How brave we were."

"You were brave, Peter. The rest of us followed like trusting children. But look. The fun starts."

They were inside the bank. In the gloom the steel doors of the vaults gleamed like an altar in a cathedral raised to Mammon. God, how formidable, Peter thought, as he studied the cone of light that surrounded the vaults. Four figures appeared abruptly, against this wall of illumination. Peter's excitement mounted; the figures became clearer as they crept stealthily toward the vaults.

"Easy now," he said quietly.

As it had been then, so it was now; tension pulled painfully at the muscles of his back while he watched the four men commence their work on the doors of the vaults.

Their figures became larger; their faces dominated the screen.

"Oh, how I loved to watch you work," Angela said. "I'm practically looking over your shoulders now."

"Don't come any closer," Peter said tensely; he was lost in time now.

"I had nothing to do on that job. So I took these pictures."

She had got the action wonderfully. There was the Irishman, lean and functional as a whip, examining the surface of the vault as an artist might a palette, wielding braces and drills like delicate brushes. While Bendell and Canalli poured liquids into test tubes, drop by drop, watching the rising vapors with narrowing eyes, their faces graven as master chefs.

Good old Bendell, Peter thought fondly. Forever worrying about trifles. Had the rain spoiled his new hat? Where were his cough drops? Did anyone remember to tip the cab driver last night? And Canalli! With the face of a gargoyle and the strength of a bull, forever in love, forever forsaken, forever forgiving. Taking the children of his mistresses for walks while the women entertained slim, boyish men who stole their money. Ah dear!

On the left side of the screen a younger Peter stood apart from the group bunched at the doors of the vault, his hands moving in gestures of encouragement, his head tilted critically, his eyes studying every move, organizing and controlling the operation like a conductor with a symphony in full cry.

The holes were punched; Bendell and Canalli moved forward, tilted their test tubes. They streaked away from the vault, merged with the darkness. Peter stared tensely at the massive doors, watched streams of vapor curling languorously from the holes circling the combination.

He began to count. "—Five! Four! Three! Two . . ."

He snapped his fingers. The vault doors buckled; a puff of smoke shot upward.

"I wish I could have got the sound," Angela said.

"There was very little," Peter said. "Just an innocent sort of thump, as a matter of fact."

The figures raced back to the vault doors. The younger Peter bent over the combination dial, his body a carving in competence. He twirled and fiddled; then with a silent cry of triumph, he pulled at the doors.

They swung open. The four men dashed into the vault.

Angela cried, "Bravo!"

The four men reappeared in what seemed a twinkling. They carried valises so stuffed with bank notes they couldn't be strapped shut; in their hands were more banknotes, thick wads of them, with satisfyingly long rows of zeros after the numerals.

Angela stretched sensuously. There was a dull, sluggish flush in her cheeks, a glaze of sweet agony in her eyes. "Mother of God, look at the money," she said. "Look at it, Francois. Look what miracles Peter can perform."

The four men filled the screen. They held packets of banknotes aloft, and their grins were wide and merry.

Peter inspected his image critically, but with an overall sense of satisfaction; he stood behind Bendell and the Irishman, not hogging the limelight, so to speak, letting them have their share of the applause. That was gracious of him, he thought, since all they did was hit their marks like well-schooled actors. Holding up the money in that fashion was a callow gesture, but on the other hand his smile was modest and his manner nearly apologetic, disclaiming, as it were, complete credit for the triumphant success of their venture. Francois turned off the projector and threw back the curtains. Peter blinked at the sunlight, reorienting himself in time; he had been out of focus for a moment,

31

drifting in a blur between past and present.

"What are you thinking of, Peter?"

She would never understand, Peter knew, so he only smiled and shook his head. Francois took a can of film from the projector and went into the bedroom. Peter was thinking fondly of his friends. They had come through, too; they were intact. Free to face whatever it pleased them to call the violet fields of peace. The Irishman in the North Counties mounting his devious, quixotic raids against the British. And Bendell, in Liege, with his flower shops, creating worlds of color and fragrance to replace those which had been destroyed for him in the war. Canalli enjoyed at last a young and loving wife, a villa ascreech with babies, and fishing boats with purple sails and holds full of sardines.

God bless them, he thought; they had all come through. There was a welling in his eyes and breast; he decided indulgently, and with some satisfaction, that he was just a sentimental ass, breaking goblets at the hearth to the memory of absent friends.

"Peter, I would hate to send that film to the police. I would hate to have to, I mean."

A wave of shock went through him. "Don't say things like that. Do you realize what would happen? In twenty-four hours Interpol would have its hand on the Irishman. On Bendell and Canalli."

"And on you, Peter."

"Well, yes. There's that, too, I suppose."

Francois came out of the bedroom, locked the door and dropped the key in his pocket. "I wouldn't get any ideas about taking it away from me," he said. "I am armed."

"Now let's get down to business," Angela said. "Unless you agree to help us, Peter, that film goes to the Interpol offices in Madrid. Tonight."

Peter studied the situation and its ramifications with care. Then he said thoughtfully, "My answer is still no. You're both frightened of something. I can smell it. I imagine the danger is quite real, and quite immediate, since you're planning something quite desperate to escape from it. But sending me to prison won't solve your problems, will it?"

"No, it won't."

"It would probably give you a certain vindictive satisfaction, but you'd still be in danger, wouldn't you?"

"That's right."

"Well then. I think I'll be on my way, Angela. If you point the finger at me, I shall point the finger at you. Then whoever you fear, or whatever you fear, will know pretty well where to find you."

"You see, Francois? I told you he was clever."

"And dangerous," Francois said, nodding gravely.

"There's one other thing," Angela said.

Peter noted with resignation the glitter of excitement in her eyes, the herringbone pattern of ski-tracks her fingernails were making on her creamy kneecaps. More aces, he thought wearily.

"Yes?"

"You'd have a hard job proving I was involved in the job at the Banco Commerciale. I was using a forged passport. Technically I never left Paris. But that's beside the point. Listen carefully: If you refuse to help us, we can't make you. But if you refuse, we will have to go to the Irishman. Or to Canalli or Bendell."

"I wish you all the luck in the world," he said drily. "They are competent mechanics. But without enough imagination among them to open a box of crackerjacks."

"But they will try."

"No. They're not fools, Angela."

She smiled at him. "But they loved you, Peter, and were grateful to you. When I tell *them* what I intend to do with the film, they won't think of themselves, but only of you. They will do anything I ask, regardless of the risk, to keep you safe and free."

The case ace, he thought bitterly; for what she said was literally true. They were staunch, loyal friends; and to such stouthearted atavisms, loyalty and friendship were not mere words, but joyous frenzies which charged their lives with meaning and excitement.

"They loved you, Peter. They would die to save you."

"And you'd use even that?"

"Make no mistake about it, Peter. I most certainly will."

Francois said: "Your refusal may well sign death warrants for your old comrades."

"And you'll go to prison, in any case," Angela said. "For I won't let you off, Peter. I'll still send the film to the police."

Well, I didn't come through after all, Peter thought, with mild wonder. There had been an interlude, a moment of grace, which he had confused with a terminal dispensation. Now he was trapped again, jailed by fears and loyalties. I've even lost the philosophical view, he thought gloomily, and somehow this was the unkindest cut of all. The most unkindest cut . . .

"Isn't there any other alternative?" he asked Angela. "I could try to raise money for you. Or maybe we could straighten out your difficulties peacefully. Robbing banks is a damned drastic business, you know."

Angela and Francois smiled and shook their heads.

"Very well," Peter said, accepting the inevitable. "I'll do what you wish. However, let's get a few things straight. If the job is theoretically possible, I'll give it a try. If not, I won't. Is that clear?"

"You'll find a way," Angela said.

"All right. One other thing. I'm to be in complete charge. One doesn't rob banks by the democratic process. I will choose the means; the time; whatever outside

35

assistance I feel is necessary. Agreed?"

"Yes, of course," Angela said. "That's precisely what we want you to do."

"One other thing," Peter said. "Now, in my presence, I want you to cover the latches on that reel of film with candle wax." He slipped off a signet ring and gave it to Angela. "Then seal it with this."

Angela smiled. "How trusting you are. But I understand."

When this was done, he said: "Now what is it you want me to steal?"

Angela told him and Peter turned quite pale.

3

ANTONIO GONZALEZ Y NAJERA, the policeman, accepted Peter's check with a gratified smile.

"You're most generous, Peter. Are you ill?"

"I beg your pardon!"

"Oh. Forgive me." Antonio laughed apologetically. "It was an unfortunate implication. Totally accidental. No. The glass of whiskey at your elbow prompted my question. Are you coming down with a cold?"

"As a matter of fact, yes."

"I was sure of it. I couldn't imagine you drinking whiskey this early in the day. You're pale, too."

"I didn't sleep well last night."

The policeman clucked sympathetically and adjusted his plump frame to a more comfortable position in the chair beside Peter's desk. "It's going around the village. I had an ache in my back this morning. And a heaviness behind my forehead. You find that a whiskey helps?"

"Oh, yes." Peter called for Mario. Whiskey was provided for the policeman.

"Ah, it seems better already."

"Mario, leave the bottle."

The policeman's mood became expansive. "The procession of the Virgins at San Fermin will be a glorious sight. Think of it. Centuries of precious stones and metals to blind the eyes of tourists. Are you going up to Pamplona for the fiesta?"

"Well, I'm not sure. Another touch?"

"If you'll join me. I think it's helping." He looked judicious. "Yes, definitely. Thank you. But you must go to Pamplona."

"If I must, I must," Peter said sighing.

"You'd better have another drink. You sound hollow. You need a holiday. I promise you this: the treasures that will adorn the Virgins of Spain at Pamplona have no equals anywhere in the world. Think of it! Precious stones and metals which haven't been displayed in public for centuries. The Contessa of Altimira's Net and Trident of diamonds, for instance. Locked away in Seville since the time of Phillip the Second. And just think! The Silver Slippers of Saint Peter will grace the feet of the Virgin of Cordoba. The Duke of Bourbon-Parma is lending the Ropes of Pearls to the Virgin from Granada. *And* the Blue Tears of Santa Eulalia. The Lacrima Christi will sparkle at the breast of Madrid's

Virgin. The Golden Oars have been promised by the House of Navarre. Barcelona is sending the Evening Stars and the Golden Bulls of the Popes of Avignon. Just a bit more, Peter. No, seriously. Only a drop. Then there will be the Diamond Flutes of Carlos . . ."

Dear God, Peter thought; the splendor of the images evoked by the policeman made him dizzy. His soul swooned as he heard in fancy the lids of all of the treasure chests in Spain slowly creaking open; as he saw through the cobwebs of time the shimmering glories of a nation's art and faith and history. The bullion of the conquistadors; the jewels of mighty monarchs; the masterworks of artisans down the centuries—all of it collected in one place at one time, all of it glowing and blazing from the statues of the Virgins at Pamplona.

The policeman was chanting on like a herald at a ball. "Isabella's coronet of diamonds; Ferdinand's Sighs of Barbara; the Marques de Santander's ruby and emerald Crown of Thorns; the platinum spark plugs from Hispana-Suiza; the—"

"What!"

"The platinum spark plugs? Oh, yes. Industry is participating, too. But they lack the baubles the old families collected over the years. So they're contributing in kind, you might say. Platinum spark plugs from Hispana-Suiza. Gold wine goblets with precious gems from the Fundador brandy people."

This seemed to remind him of something; he looked

in mild wonder at his empty glass. Peter filled it.

"Oh, thank you." The policeman sighed and crossed his booted feet at the ankles. "I find it all very confusing, Peter." He sipped his drink. "Once there was a nice division of activity between the north and south of Spain. We sold the tourists—as it were—gypsies, bandits, romance, tall tales." He laughed softly. "Ah, yes . . . maidens fleeing from storm devils. Their little nipples pinched by the hot fingers of ogres riding the west wind. It went over nicely with tourists. The north, on the other hand, sold good plumbing, comfortable hotels, and shops full of handbags and brass candlesticks. And that went over nicely too. But now the north wants to borrow our poverty and mix it up with their coal mines and real estate."

Peter's head was beginning to ache.

"Peter, let me give you a recipe for a tourist boom. Only one thing is necessary. Comfortable seats from which visitors may examine the edifying old virtues of hunger and poverty. That is the only reason the administration of Pamplona has invited our little peasant Virgin to the Fiesta. Amidst the splendor of the grand Virgins, poor little Santa Maria with her cracked eyeball and broken fingers will provide the touch of poverty which is essential to the contentment of tourists. They must have someone to pity; someone to patronize. That is all we are providing. I ache with the shame of it, Peter."

The maids had been sniffling about the same thing this morning, Peter recalled; Santa Maria had nothing to wear to the ball. Only seed pearls and tarnished bracelets.

Peter's phone rang. It was Grace.

"You didn't come by last night, Peter. Are you sulking?"

"No, of course not."

"Not about my children? Or the other thing?"

"No."

"Then why did you stand me up?"

"I had a cold. I went to bed."

"How very prudent of you!"

The phone clicked in his ear.

The policeman had not stopped talking. "Of course they won't admit it. They discussed the security regulations with me quite gravely. Just as if our poor Virgin owned anything worth stealing." He laughed and poured himself Scotch. "This might interest you, Peter. All the treasures will be kept in one bank. And that bank was chosen by lot. Interesting? Guess what bank they chose?"

"Antonio, I don't think you should tell me."

The policeman looked blank. "Why not?"

"Obviously it's a matter of security."

"Ha, ha. You don't want to be tempted, eh?" The policeman laughed heartily; Peter's headache grew worse. "No, I trust you, Peter. The treasures will be kept in the vaults of the Banco de Bilbao. In all seriousness, that is a secret. But it doesn't matter. There is no point to robbing banks in Spain."

"You're quite sure of that?"

"Oh, yes. Remember when those Greeks stole the money from the Bánco de Navarre? The Guardia Civil apprehended them on the road to Algeciras. They formed a semicircle about the car, machine-gunned the occupants to death. Fortunately, they were indeed the culprits. Examples of that sort, plus the fact that the garotte is used in capital crimes, encourages criminals to take a prudent view of things. They can rob and steal with great confidence in other countries. But they stay out of Spain. Look at Aristide Broualt, for example. One of the most formidable thieves to ever operate in Europe. Correct?"

"Well, I suppose so. But there was something vulgar about him, I felt."

"Notifying the police in advance, that sort of thing? Well, perhaps you're right. But he was enormously clever. And yet, he never tried his tricks in Spain. Nor did the one the papers dubbed the Ace of Diamonds."

"Frankly, Antonio, as a policeman, didn't you find him rather tiresome? Take that playing card and stiletto he always left at the scene of the crime! With gryphons drawn on it! Trademarks are childish, to start with. But theatrical ones are downright embarrassing."

"Yes, I agree. But the custom is an ancient one. Perhaps he was an old man. But young or old, he kept out of Spain. And so did Christopher Page, the Englishman. They were wise, Peter. Jimmy Fingers, Karl Maganer, and the one they called the Count of Soho—they were supreme in their line of work, but they all stayed out of Spain."

"Supreme? That's an interesting point. Would you say, for instance, they were more accomplished than the American, Stuart Carmichael?"

"Oh, definitely, Peter. Definitely."

"Then how about the Black Dove?"

"The Black Dove?" The policeman frowned and shook his head slowly. "The Black Dove? I don't recall that one. Was he a man or a woman?"

"You must remember, Antonio. Think, for heaven's sake."

"I have just a vague memory."

"The Banco Commerciale in Lisbon. The Credit Lyonaise in Paris. The Nationale in Rome. To name only a few."

"Oh, yes, yes," Antonio said. "I remember now."

"I should rather think you would."

"Yes, the Black Dove. A clever one. But again, Peter, he never set foot in Spain. But this is idle talk. No intelligent person would bother stealing the jewels from the Virgins."

43

"Why do you say 'bother'?"

"Because they are priceless; therefore worthless."

That was neatly put, Peter thought with a touch of envy. He might have used it in his journal. Things beyond value have no value. Or something like that. But the policeman's was better. The jewels were priceless; therefore worthless. He wondered if Angela had considered that.

Antonio stood with care. "I must be going." He looked through his pockets. "By the way, I found your parking summons. Lucky thing, eh?"

"Oh, yes."

"Peter, you're pale. You don't look well. I'd have a drink, if I were you."

He went fluidly through the door. Peter sighed and put his fingertips to his temples. Then he frowned faintly, and considered the policeman's last words. At last he began to smile. Relief flooded through him, sluicing away his headache. Scooping up the phone he dialed the Pez Espada.

"Angela? I've got to see you and Francois. Immediately."

"Is anything wrong?"

"I've got ghastly news."

He hung up on a hiss of angry questions. Smiling thoughtfully, Peter strolled to the bar and told Mario he wanted a whiskey. Reconsidering, he said, "Better make it a double."

44

On the terrace of Peter's Bar, Mr. Shahari was explaining the rate to an American named Morgan and an Englishman named Quince, while under their table a mongrel dog fed on peanuts and the husks of shrimp.

"Yes, the rate of exchange is sixty-seven in Tangier, Mr. Morgan. You've got it quite right. It is sixty-nine in Fez, as a matter of fact. And in Dakar it is even higher. But, unfortunately, here on the southern coast of Spain it is only fifty-eight."

Morgan was an uncommonly fat young man with a round vulnerable face, a huge blond beard, and eyes that were clear and blue and wholly mad.

"Wherever you go the rate drops," he cried wrathfully.

"But I have nothing to do with the rate!" Mr. Shahari exclaimed in mild surprise. The Indian was small, neatly dressed, and he glittered; his spectacles, his fountain pens, his rings, his gold teeth, all sparkled brightly in the clear sunlight. "The rate is a constant, Mr. Morgan."

"Then why is it always changing? Why am I always getting screwed by it?" The mountainous ranges of fat on Morgan's ribs trembled indignantly. "Just tell me that!"

"The rate in one place is not the same as the rate in another place," Mr. Shahari explained with an air of exhaustive lucidity. "Now. How many dollars do you wish to exchange?"

"All I've got. Twenty-eight."

"Mr. Quince?"

"I've got twelve pound ten."

Quince was as thin as Morgan was fat. A thoughtful man, one of his favorite fancies was to imagine what might happen if a group of mice learned how to link arms. Might they then attack rats?

Mr. Shahari counted out pesetas, collected dollars and pounds in return, moved to another table. Morgan stared after him furiously. Strange wild thoughts blew about inside his head.

"I'd like to kill him," he said to Quince. "There's the true evil of the world. The middleman. Clipping a fat profit from both sides of every deal. In Hong Kong, Calcutta, Tanger, Paris; they're everywhere. Stealing our money whenever we cross a border. They'll have it all one of these days."

"Now then, Ah wouldn't kill 'im," Quince said thoughtfully. "Ah wouldn't do that. Cause a bloody row, it would."

"It wouldn't be a murder; it would be an execution." Morgan's excitement grew; his mad eyes sparkled happily. "It should be in public; with crowds to witness it. In a mood of holiday, of fiesta. Amidst music and fireworks, Mr. Shahari should be terminally collected for his sins against humanity. Don't you think that would be appropriate?"

"Ah wouldn't execute 'im either," Quince said doubtfully. "Cause a bloody row, it would."

Morgan smiled at clouds that were like wisps of cotton on the horizon, and called up a vision of Biblical retribution and justice, which was tinged, however, with respectable existential overtones. Pamplona? He nodded slowly, his chins rising and falling like pneumatic shock absorbers. Appropriate, he thought, most appropriate.

"Angela, I simply cannot do it," Peter said. "It's not a matter of spirit, but of flesh. You commented on my drinking yesterday. You asked if it were something new. I wish to God it were. But it's been going on for years. And lately it's been accelerating at a cyclical rate of increase. Francois, give me a glass of whiskey. One ice cube, if you will."

Peter paced the floor of their suite, his eyes rolling about in his head, his movements jerky and erratic. "Just look at my hands! Do you remember how I used to take watches apart without tools? I tried it last night. It was ghastly! Screws and wheels clattering all over the place."

"I think you're lying, Peter."

"Why should I lie about it? I've deteriorated badly, Angela. Would *you* like your life hanging on my skills? My reflexes? They're shot, I tell you. Gone."

Francois did something unexpected then, something which rather surprised Peter. He took a revolver from

47

his pocket and swung the butt in a vicious arc at Peter's head.

Peter thought fleetingly of defending himself with a basic judo take-down which would in all likelihood have broken the Frenchman's wrist and elbow. But he decided against this. He moved his head and let the gun butt whistle by. As Francois lost his balance, Peter plucked the gun from his hand and spun him into a chair.

"Now that was very stupid," he said quietly. "I dislike physical violence." Peter broke the gun, knocked the bullets from its chambers. "Let me tell you something, Francois. If you ever try anything that silly again, I shall pound one of these bullets up each of your nostrils. It's the quickest and most painful way to deviate a septum I know of."

Francois was smiling. So was Angela.

"I was only checking your reflexes," Francois said casually.

"Oh," Peter said. Fool, fool, *fool!* he thought.

Francois stood and took the revolver from Peter. "Give me the bullets."

Angela said mildly, "Peter, that wasn't like you. It was extremely foolish. Please don't make us impatient with you. Remember your friends."

That night Peter wrote gloomily in his journal: *Do not feel antagonistic toward people who are cleverer than you. They may have advantages you lack: i.e., brains.*

That wasn't too bad, he decided. The aptness of the phrasing cheered him; it lay like balm on his wounded ego. He continued writing. *The superior person is always surrounded by inferiors; that is the curse of excellence. How trying it must be for God! To look down and find everyone on his knees! Begging favors. Give me money, God. Please don't let them score, God. I don't want to be pregnant, God, I'm a good girl. But did God listen?*

That was a scary notion.

Of course He listens. What else does He have to do? God is love and grace. The association tempted him toward cliffs of blasphemy. Slowly he wrote: *God is Grace.* But the words seemed to form a happy union, innocent of disrespect or cheekiness. *God is trumpets and bugles,* he wrote. *God is surrender. God is cellos.*

Made whole again by these annealing reflections, Peter raised a glass of brandy to his reflection in the mirror above the fireplace. "They have heard the lion whimper," he said. "Now they shall hear him roar."

"Que dice, senor?"

"Nothing, Adela, nothing at all," he said to the maid who stood in the doorway. She went away frowning.

Peter picked up the telephone and called the Pez Espada.

"Pepe, this is Senor Churchman. Listen. Monsieur

and Madame Morel. Is there any way you can get them out of their rooms for about half an hour?"

"But of course, Peter. I shall tell them the suite needs to be fumigated."

"Perfect. Will you do it right away?"

"Of course, Peter." There was a pause. "Is that all?"

"Yes. And thank you, Pepe."

Peter fancied he heard a sigh as he replaced the receiver in its cradle.

Morgan found Mr. Shahari in a bar on the beach. The Indian was tallying his scores. Stacks of checks and bills covered the table.

"Well, this is a break. Mind if I sit down?"

"I'm busy, Mr. Morgan."

"I wondered. Are you going up to Pamplona?"

Morgan sank into a chair. The swell of his vast stomach caused the table to rise and tilt mysteriously, as it might have under the hands of a swami at a seance. "Watch it," he said.

Mr. Shahari clutched at checks and bills. "No, I am not going to Pamplona, Mr. Morgan."

"Well, what if I have to change some money? There's a pound note behind your chair, I think."

Mr. Shahari's voice came from beneath the table. "How much do you have to change?"

"Well, right now, nothing. But next week I'll have quite a lot."

Mr. Shahari's head rose in the air. Morgan's stomach swelled once more and drove the edge of the table against the Indian's gullet.

"Damn, I'm sorry. Watch those checks."

"How much will you have to change?" Mr. Shahari said hoarsely.

"They've just settled my father's estate. I get twenty thousand dollars next week."

Mr. Shahari made it his business to know bits and pieces about his clients; even such a little fish as Morgan, whose father he knew to be an international lawyer of formidable reputation, and to be—if last week's issue of *Time* could be trusted—in excellent heath.

"I congratulate you, Mr. Morgan. Good-bye."

"Then you're not going up to Pamplona?"

"Most certainly not. Good-bye."

Morgan confided his disappointment to Quince. "It's just that he doesn't trust me, you see. But he'll come all right. If someone he knows has money. That's what's so flawless about it. So perfect. A symbol of greed annihilated by greed. You've got to help me, Quince."

"Take my word, Morgan. Killin' 'im will cause an awful bloody row. It will get around, you know."

In dark slacks and a black shirt Peter drifted like a shadow to the side of the Pez Espada which faced the sea. In the parking lot on the other side of the hotel, car doors slammed and high-pitched laughter came floating through the night. Music rose and fell in tinkling loops.

The first-floor terrace was three feet above Peter's head. He crouched, measured the distance, sprang upward through the darkness. His hands caught the edge of the terrace. He secured his grip, chinned himself, swung up on top of the railing which rimmed the terrace. Balancing himself, Peter peered into a room in which a tall man with a cold face was practicing putting.

The man tapped a golf ball toward a mechanical gadget six feet away. The ball disappeared into a hole, popped out, and rolled back to him. Clever, Peter thought. The man sank nine putts in a row. The tenth hung on the rim of the hole. The man stamped on the floor. With a glance over his shoulder, he strolled to the gadget, his putter swinging casually. He tapped the ball in without looking at it. A woman appeared in the bedroom door.

"Ten in a row, dear," he said.

"Wonderful."

Peter leaped up through the darkness. On the second floor an American couple played backgammon. On the third, an elderly woman in a bathrobe scolded a small dog. The room on the fourth floor was dark. God bless Pepe, Peter thought, as he swung lightly over the railing.

He let himself into Angela's suite and moved silently to the bedroom. From his hand a beam of light probed

52

the darkness like a slender lance. It took him only a few minutes to check the closets, drawers, and luggage. He noticed a steamer trunk at the foot of the bed. A hasp and combination lock secured its lid.

Peter settled himself before the trunk, rubbed his hands together to warm them, then began delicately to manipulate the dial on the lock. The tumblers fell with no more sound than feathers on velvet, but to Peter's sensitive fingertips they were noisy as castanets.

Smiling, he opened the lock, raised the lid of the trunk.

Something cold touched his temple.

"Get up," Francois said.

Light flooded the room. Peter swiveled his eyes sideways and saw the muzzle of Francois's revolver inches from his head.

"Peter, I'm becoming very cross with you," Angela said.

Peter stood slowly, remembering Pepe's sigh and cursing himself for a bloody fool.

Angela stood in the doorway to the living room. She wore a short, ice-blue evening dress, and slippers with rhinestone heels. Under the shining cap of black hair, her face was white with anger.

"You look very smart, I must say," Peter said.

"This is your last chance, Peter. Your very last."

Francois wore a dinner jacket. Peter didn't like the fear and anger in his eyes, nor the way his knuckles had

53

whitened on the butt of the gun.

"Don't kill him, Francois," Angela said quietly.

"Tell me why not? He's no good to us. We returned to our room, found a prowler, I shot him. Tell me why that isn't the intelligent thing to do! The only thing to do, as a matter of fact."

"Peter, will you give me your word? No more tricks?"

"I have no choice."

"San Fermin starts a week today. Will you promise to go to Pamplona tomorrow and look things over?"

"Yes."

"Will you promise to do exactly what you agreed to yesterday?"

"I promise."

Francois looked at her angrily. "And you'll take his word?"

"I should have thought of it before. He is very serious about promises. Aren't you, Peter?"

"It all comes down to how one was brought up, I imagine."

"Then I have your word. No more tricks."

"You have my word."

"This seems too simple," Francois said drily. The gun in his hand was still aimed at Peter's belt buckle. "He gives us a promise like a Boy Scout, and then everything is all right. Mr. Churchman, listen to me: Angela is after money, but I am fighting to save my life. There's a difference. I hope you understand it."

There was a subtle change in the Frenchman's manner now, and Peter attempted to assay it with care and accuracy, for his instincts warned him of danger. The gun, that was it; the gun made the difference. It gave him weight and substance. Until this moment Peter had looked through Francois as he would a pane of glass. But now he fancied he saw something alive and sinister at work behind the greedy eyes, the pointlessly handsome features. The potential of the gun seemed to magnify Francois in an odd fashion; in this new dimension the very neutrality and ordinariness of his features became a fact of curious significance.

Peter said: "I'm going to do all I can to save my friends, you can be sure of that. I've given you my word; I'll try my best. That's all I can promise you, now isn't it?"

"Let me give you a promise in return," Francois said quietly. "If you don't get what we want, I'll kill you. Is that clear?"

"Oh, yes. And I'll certainly keep it in mind. Goodnight, Angela."

In the lobby Peter listened ruefully to Pepe. "They were suspicious when I told them it would be necessary to fumigate their rooms. They offered me money."

Peter sighed. "And I didn't. It was stupid of me, Pepe. I forgot. I'm sorry."

"That's all right, Senor Churchman."

"It wasn't intentional, you realize. No hard feelings?"

"Of course not. Such things shouldn't come between friends."

"Good night, Pepe."

"Good night, Senor Churchman."

In a chair near the entrance to the hotel, a tall and formidably proportioned man in a black raincoat lowered his newspaper and watched Peter pass through the revolving doors. Then he popped a mint into his mouth and sucked on it. There was an odd lack of animation in his face and eyes; like a sluggish, heavy animal behind a fence, he seemed to regard the world without interest or curiosity. He might have been thirty or forty; his blond hair was clipped short, and his eyes were clear and patient under a pattern of scars that were drawn on his forehead as precisely as the lines in a tick-tack-toe game. When he stood, however, slapping the newspaper under his arm and stepping out toward the information desk, it was evident he had been trained to handle his big body with economy and precision. At the counter, he smiled at Pepe, and said in careful, unaccented English: "The man you were speaking with a moment ago—can you tell me something about him?"

He analyzed Pepe's expression and drew out a wallet.

Peter went home and drank four large brandies before going to bed. As sleep began to circle him like a

vast but silent typhoon, he wondered drowsily if the
film had really and truly been hidden in Angela's
steamer trunk. It made very little difference one way
or the other now, but he disliked not knowing; it nagged
at him. Ask Angela? No. No good. Go back and take
another look? No. There was his promise. . . . No
more tricks.

"God help me," he murmured despairingly and fell
asleep.

Peter tried valiantly the following morning. He rose,
showered, brushed his teeth, thought calmly of what
lay ahead of him, and then went wearily back to bed.

Much later came soft footsteps, an aroma of coffee.

"Take it away, Adela. Please."

"It's not Adela, it's me," Grace said. "May I open the
curtains?"

"Good God, no."

"What's the matter, Peter? Why are you avoiding
me?"

The bed sank slightly with her weight. Waves of
sluggish liquids sloshed about in Peter's head.

"It has nothing to do with you, darling."

"It's cruel of you not to tell me what's wrong."

He turned his head. She sat on the edge of the bed,
her back hollowed out as if she were on a show horse.
She wore a white dress and her shoulders were bare. In
the gloom she towered above him like a lovely iceberg

floating serenely on dark polar seas.

"I'm desperate," he said.

"I feel so helpless. Do you want to go to bed with me?"

"No, darling." This was a first, he realized with a touch of panic. He felt his head. "Have I gone bald, by any chance?"

"Of course not, you silly man. What ever gave you that idea? Anyway, if you comb it sideways, no one would notice such a little spot. Not for years."

God, he thought. The bad things were happening at last. He saw himself locked in a prison cell, impotent, bald as an egg.

"Please tell me why you're acting so strangely. I can't bear to see you like this."

Peter looked into her splendid loving eyes, luminous now with unshed tears, and came to a decision: He told her everything.

"What a horrid little bitch this Angela must be! Would she really throw your old friends to the wolves?"

"She most certainly would!"

"Peter, you aren't pulling my leg, are you?"

"Damn it, of course not!"

"Seriously. You went about Europe breaking into banks, stealing all kinds of money?"

"In England too."

"But why? And please don't say because they were

there. You must have had a good reason."

"Of course. I wanted the money."

"Peter, you're teasing me. I'm really curious."

He managed to sip some coffee. Since he had gone this far, there seemed no point in not making a clean breast of things.

"All right. I've never told anyone before. And I'd appreciate it if you'd keep all this to yourself. It makes me appear an even greater fool than I actually am." He sighed. "During the war I bombed a cathedral by mistake. It was at night so I didn't kill anybody. But I felt terrible about it. I couldn't get over it. Such staggering carelessness. It preyed on my mind. Imagine how you'd feel if you ran through a red light and killed Albert Schweitzer! Or dropped a Sèvres bowl and smashed it to bits! Well, I felt even worse."

"Oh, darling, I do love you. I can imagine how you must have felt. But aren't you being too hard on yourself? It was wartime. You were flying a mission. You were over enemy territory."

"No. I was returning from a mission. I was over Manchester, as a matter of fact."

She sighed. "Well, I suppose that makes a difference."

"It was eight hundred years old," he said gloomily. "It had taken three generations of laborers and artisans to build it. I found all this out later, of course. They all had to go to confession before starting work in the

morning. Each stone was put in place by men with theoretically spotless souls. Think of it! Then I fly by,
mooning about steaks and beer and girls, and drop a
bomb on it. The bomb-release mechanism is secured by
throwing a switch to the right. To the *right!* That's
printed in block capitals in the manual. I yawned and
threw it to the left. My silly name made it all the more
ghastly."

"I don't understand."

"Churchman. Peter *Churchman.* I'm not particularly
religious or anything. But something is definitely wrong
when a man named Churchman destroys a cathedral.
It made me feel the butt end of a very stupid joke, I
can tell you."

"You poor dear. Only an exquisite sort of person
would grieve about a thing like that."

"Well, I decided to send them a contribution. It
seemed the least I could do. I went into business, at
which I was no good at all. Then I had an inspiration. I
saved some money and tried my luck at Monte Carlo. I
didn't see how I could miss. I was doing the Lord's
work. God was my partner. But I lost every dime. And I
never heard from God at all."

She smiled and touched his cheek. "He was a silent
partner, darling."

Peter felt a stab of envy. How nicely that would have
looked in his journal! The irrelevance of his thoughts
depressed him, for he knew at heart he wasn't a serious

man; in the profound recesses of his being there sat a child grinning at comic books.

"I do understand now," she said gently. "You robbed the banks to pay for the cathedral."

"Yes. I deducted only my expenses. Of course, I had no way of determining the value of a cathedral. Costs have risen a lot since it was built, you know. But I settled on a million dollars. I collected that and sent it to the City Council of Manchester, with my apologies."

"Oh, Peter. Did you tell them who you were or anything?"

"I couldn't do that. I just said it was from a repentant airman, and hoped they realized it had been a mistake and so forth."

The light in her eyes was like a bonfire whipped by high winds, splendid and exciting.

"Darling, how magnificent!"

He moved her dress and kissed her bare knees. Suddenly he felt much better; confession had eased his soul. He listened to the mounting tempo of his heart, and decided that things were quite all right again. Things were unbelievably good once more, he realized, as his fingertips slowly rounded the delicious curves of her legs.

"Darling, lock the door."

"Why?"

"I would love to merge with the infinite."

"Oh, how sweetly you put things."

61

She locked the door, undid straps and stepped from her dress and sandals. The light in the room was the color of pearls now, the color of southern seas at dawn, and through this shimmering translucence she came to Peter like a stately white clipper under gentle homing winds.

Mr. Shahari fled up an alley. Morgan cunningly plotted his probable course, waddled along side streets and caught him near the church square.

"Now look. About my father. I got that wrong. It was my uncle who died. But I'll have the money next week. There's no doubt of that. None at all."

"I wish you happiness with it. But I am not going to Pamplona. This is my area. This is where I work."

"Ah, come on. You'll have fun." Morgan winked and moved closer to Mr. Shahari. "Let me tell you about the girls who come down from Biarritz."

Mr. Shahari backed away from the vast rounded prow of Morgan's stomach. He sat down abruptly in the burros' drinking fountain.

"Damn you, great fat fool! No, no, no."

Morgan told Quince about it later. "He put on a good act, but he's got the hook in his mouth. He'll come to Pamplona, don't worry. And there we shall kill him, eh Quince? With ritual and spectacle, eh Quince?"

Quince was silent. He believed he had already expressed himself more than adequately on this subject.

4 ∿

PETER WORKED with speed and precision in Pamplona.
Time was his challenge and his enemy, but he deliberately made himself stand apart and examine the problem from a viewpoint that was nearly academic in its
detachment and serenity. He analyzed possibilities and
calculated risks with surgical dispassion; this had always been his great strength, this ability to choose
plans as if they were going to be executed by robots
while he himself was off taking the sun on safe and
distant beaches.

He would have liked weeks to study this job. Instead
he had only days, only hours, to decide on a scheme
that might save his old friends from Angela's reprisals.
No, he couldn't be choosy; Peter was quite willing in
fact to settle for anything that was not demonstrably
suicidal.

He gave a list of things he might need to the desk clerk at his hotel.

"Yes, senor. I'll attend to it. Street maps. And films of San Fermin. Yes, I can have them sent over from the photographer's shop."

"I'll also need a sixteen millimeter projector and screen."

"I'll attend to everything."

"You're very kind."

"It's a pleasure, senor. Since you love San Fermin as I do, we must be *compadres*."

"I was only here once and I did love it. But that was long ago."

"Never mind. The pictures will bring it all back. And time stands still for those with passion."

"Thank you. That's a comforting thought. Will you send the things up to my room, please?"

"I'll take care of everything, senor."

"Thank you so much."

The clerk beamed after Peter: it was a pleasure to serve a gentleman, a *compadre*. Such a rare pleasure.

Ten minutes later Peter sat across a desk from an officer of the Banco de Bilbao.

"I don't much like the idea of opening an account in Spain, Senor Galache. You never know what can happen. It's like South America. But I've got to. Tell me: You got a statement of your current financial position?"

"But of course, Mr. Clay."

"Okay." Peter accepted a booklet, put it away in his pocket without looking at it. "Now, you got any banking facilities in the Far East?"

"Yes. In Hong Kong. May I ask the nature of your business, Mr. Clay?"

"Heavy equipment. Earth movers, cranes, bulldozers, that sort of thing. Your vault's from Samsons in London, I see. It's the old Model X-fifty, I suppose."

"No, it's rather more modern. It's the X-one hundred."

"Yeah? Well, I'll look at your statement. If it's all right, I'll be back after lunch."

"Are you staying in Pamplona for the Fiesta of San Fermin?"

"No."

"That's a pity. It's very colorful. Since you're right here, why not wait over till next week?"

"Next week? Hell, I'll be in Calcutta then."

The Spaniard thought: I don't care where you will be, Mr. Clay. Leave your American dollars but take your American manners far away.

"In that case, may I wish you a pleasant trip?"

"Sure. So long."

Peter disliked the role he had played; it made him quite gloomy, in fact. That it had been necessary hardly made it more agreeable. Peter had forced the pleasant young Spaniard to concentrate on his bad manners, so that he wouldn't wonder at his questions about the number and model of the bank vaults. Clever, oh yes, he thought. But he didn't enjoy behaving like that. He sighed and wondered if he had become too sensitive for this sort of work.

For the next few hours Peter strolled leisurely about the town, deliberately absorbing its texture and atmosphere. This seemingly aimless tour was essential to his preparations, and he knew from experience it wouldn't pay to hurry it; time was precious, but so was information about which way the streets ran, and where the policemen stood at given hours, and when the crowds would be thickest in the squares and market places.

He liked the old Basque stronghold. He liked its yellow buildings and stone fortifications, its avenues and monuments, and the briskly sturdy look of its people. He found the street of the Thousand-Broken-Heads where Ignatius of Loyola had received the wound that turned his steps and reflections to sainthood, and he carefully measured and studied the Calle de la Estafeta, through which the foolhardy and courageous of all ages would run before the *encierros* of bulls each morning during the fiesta of San Fermin.

Peter stopped for a glass of beer at one of the cafés that ringed the Plaza de Castillo. The great square was now quiet and orderly but next week it would be the joyously thumping heart of the fiesta; thronged with dancers, musicians, merrymakers; trembling with the explosions of rockets and fireworks; all the cafés mobbed, every table sprouting thick clusters of bottles and glasses and saucers.

After a bit Peter left some coins for the waiter and went back to his hotel.

At the wheel of a gray Citroen parked in the Plaza de Castillo, a man in a black raincoat looked after Peter with a frown that delicately rearranged the pattern of scars on his forehead. Seated beside him was a short stocky man with silvery white hair and features so hard and seasoned that they might have been hacked from a block of mahogany.

The man in the black raincoat said, "I don't understand it, sir. He's drifting about like a tourist."

"Not quite, Phillip. Tourists shop for things. Postcards, souvenirs, and so forth. Not Mr. Churchman. He is looking at things. And looking very carefully."

"I see. That didn't occur to me, Colonel."

"Well, I was paid to notice such things, and you weren't, Phillip."

"Yes, Colonel."

"Please, Phillip. That's all over."

"It's difficult, sir. It's a strong habit, sir."

"Would it help if I made it a direct order?"

"Yes, I'm sure it would, Colonel."

"Do not address me by rank again, Sergeant Lemoins. That is an order."

"Very well, sir."

The Colonel glanced at his watch. "We must talk to Mr. Churchman soon. But first I suggest we have our lunch. Did you like the place called The Four Crowns?"

"Very much, sir."

"Then let's go there, Phillip."

"Yes, Colonel."

Peter spent much of that afternoon in his darkened hotel room studying films taken the previous year during the fiesta of San Fermin. He watched daredevils in the Calle de las Estefeta fleeing before fighting bulls; saw amateur *toreros* caping bony and frantic young oxen in the Plaza de Toros; followed snake-lines of exuberant dancers looping and curling through the crowds in the Plaza de Castillo.

Something else caught his eye and he quickly stopped the action on the screen.

High above the crowds in the Plaza de Castillo floated gigantic heads, their mouths stretched wide in fiercely cheerful smiles.

Peter studied them intently, while a tantalizingly amorphous idea began to take shape in his mind. He remembered those huge, gaily painted heads from his first visit to Pamplona. And what else? Did time really stand still for those with passion? He remembered the bulls and the fireworks and the men dancing in the streets, the bad news on the radio and the goatskins of wine raised high through all the reeling night, the funny, unpronounceable names of the towns in Poland, and a sudden wistful knowledge that passion and excitement died with the loss of innocence.

He was oddly disturbed by his memories. Very well, he thought sadly, let the innocent weep for such things; sinners know the value of peace and a bottle of good wine.

He made himself concentrate on the heads. They were called *Cabezudas,* he remembered, or *Gigantes.* Peter stood abruptly, as if physical activity might be a specific against his strange gloom, and measured the heads immobilized on the screen. As nearly as he could judge—by using the human figures in the scene as a scale—the eyes of the *Cabezudas* were ten or twelve feet above the ground, and their foreheads were about three feet wide. The heads were constructed, it appeared, of lacquered cloth or leather stretched around wooden frames. The men who supported them were concealed by flowing robes which dropped from the shoulders of the *Cabezudas.* Eyeholes cut in the cloth allowed the men to guide themselves safely through the streets. For several minutes Peter stared at the silent screen, a frown shadowing his eyes. He was wondering how much strength and stamina one would require to carry a *Cubezuda* about the city for an hour or so. . . .

At last he rose and made himself a drink. Gripped by mounting excitement, he paced the floor and stared at the grinning heads frozen on the screen. An idea flickered and danced about the dark corners of his mind like a will-o-the-wisp. It was so audacious that his first impulse was to put it straight from his mind, to fling it away as he would a ticking bomb.

But this element was precisely what appealed to Peter, for his strange genius warned him that the problem he faced could not be solved by prudent and cautious means. In such a situation, danger was often the finest camouflage. Peter respected the police of all countries profoundly; otherwise he would have been in prison long ago. But he knew from experience that the police at times fell into the error of confusing the criminal mind with their own, declaring, in effect: "Only a fool would take such a chance!" What they forgot, or had never known, was that men and women who went about breaking into banks and museums *were* fools, and quite naturally should be expected to behave like fools. Words such as "suicidal" and "foolhardy" and "impregnable" were frequently the thief's most valuable ally, for they created the climate of official complacence in which the seeds of a plan might sprout, undetected and unsuspected, into lovely and profitable blooms.

No, Peter thought, danger was an asset. The problem was timing! How to mesh frail and erratic human nerves and reflexes with the impersonal, inexorable sweep of a second hand. . . .

Stimulated by the challenge to his professional skills,

Peter put his glass aside, scooped up his hat, and left the room.

Twenty minutes later he stood in the gathering darkness near a bridge and looked across the river toward the corrals of the bulls. Lights winked below him on the sluggish water. The area was now deserted and quiet; only an occasional worker strolled by to break the stillness with the damp and hollow ring of boots on the old cobblestones.

Peter stood with a stopwatch in his hand, and allowed his formidable imagination to create pictures against the night. How would it be next week during the fiesta of San Fermin? The hands of an official would grip a plunger, while his eye watched a second hand sweeping toward six o'clock. At the stroke of the hour a deep, booming roar would shake the city. Birds would fly screaming from the spires and steeples of the churches, and the runners packed in the Calle de la Estefeta would know that the fighting bulls had been released from their corrals.

Peter imagined the seven dark shapes trotting out to a false freedom in the early dawn, their shoulder muscles cresting ominously as they shadowboxed the air with lethal horns. Flanked by massive, imperturbable oxen, the bulls would quickly calm down and bunch themselves into a protective *encierro;* in this fashion they would begin their race through the barricaded streets to the appointed place of their execution that afternoon, the Plaza de Toros at the foot of the Calle de la Estefeta.

The instant they formed an *encierro* and started running, a second blast would shake the city; and the daredevils in the streets would know that the bulls were loose and on their way.

Peter clicked his stopwatch, turned, and sprinted up the street. The first stretch was a difficult two hundred yards over treacherous cobblestones to the small plaza in front of the Ayuntamento, Pamplona's city hall. Arriving there, Peter leaned against a wall to catch his breath, and waved off sympathetic offers of aid from several concerned Spaniards. Then he looked at his stopwatch. It would be tight, very tight, he realized grimly.

He inspected the plaza. During the running of the bulls all its openings and passageways would be sealed off with double wooden barriers. Every window with a view of the square would be packed with faces; crowds would throng the top of the barricades; the square itself would be occupied by a few dozen *suicideros*, those insanely courageous, or insanely neurotic, young men who would not take to their heels until they actually saw the bulls thundering up that two-hundred yard stretch from the riverbanks.

Fortunately, considering certain elements of his plans, Peter was quite certain that no one in the crowd would have eyes or thoughts for anything but the arrival of those bulls. The noise would mount in wild waves, and these would break into sheer pandemonium when the first dark and murderous shapes topped the rise of the street and exploded into the plaza.

And that was fine, Peter thought.

He strolled across the square and went into a passageway between two buildings. It was narrow and dark and damp, and smelled of rust and old mortar. Peter played the beam of his flashlight over doors and windows. Moisture glistened slickly on the walls. The noise of the town was muted and indistinct; the passageway was like a narrow tomb stretching off to a gloomy infinity.

Peter felt the old excitement creeping over him. Steel bars and vaults were a gauntlet flung in his face, a challenge he couldn't resist. He went carefully along the passageway until he came to a solid brick wall. There was no turning right or left. This was the end. The windows at the base of the wall were guarded with clusters of iron grillwork. Peter inspected them carefully under the beam of his torch, programming their measurements into data for the computers in his mind. But even as he worked he experienced a certain sadness, a certain guilty gloom, for he realized now how much he had missed this sort of thing, and how pleased and excited he was to be back at it. And he couldn't help wondering if he had really been honest about wanting to make restitution for the colossal error he had committed during the war. Or had he simply been rationalizing a need to steal? Or to prove, perhaps, that he was cleverer than the police?

Suddenly Peter blinked in surprise. He had always been vain about his eyesight, which was like that of eagles, but now, of all times, it appeared to be letting him down.

For there seemed to be two beams of light crisscrossing the barred windows at the base of the wall.

"Have you lost something, senor?"

Peter turned, smiling blankly. The second beam of light moved up to his face. The man directing it at him was a policeman. Peter had a shadowy impression of brass buttons, red epaulets, a young unsmiling face.

"As a matter of fact, I seem to have lost my way."

"What address were you looking for?"

"Well, I don't know. I'm trying to find the Banco de Bilbao. Someone told me it was near here."

"He misinformed you, I'm afraid."

"Perhaps I misunderstood."

"Yes, that's possible. You realize the Banco de Bilbao is closed?"

"Yes, I know. But I wanted to find it so I could get there first thing in the morning."

The policeman smiled. "You're not far from it right now." He rapped his knuckles against the brick wall. "It's on the other side of this building. Twenty or thirty feet away."

"Is that so?"

"Yes. But unless you can walk through solid walls, I don't think that will help very much."

Peter smiled too. "No indeed."

The policeman embroidered his little joke. "And I don't imagine you'd want to buy some dynamite and blast your way into the bank."

"No, I certainly wouldn't."

The policeman took Peter's arm and led him back along the passageway to the square. "In that case, I think the best thing would be to walk around the block. You'll be at the doors of the Banco de Bilbao in a matter of minutes."

"Well, thanks very much. And good night."

"It's nothing, senor. Good night."

The policeman, whose name was Carlos, smiled after Peter. Tourists never seemed to be at home, he reflected philosophically. Always losing their way, forever straying into strange places, and then smiling like shy children, like naughty children, when someone set them straight. With a tolerant shrug, Carlos turned and strolled off in the opposite direction, hands clasped behind his back, his clear dark eyes alertly roving the streets for anything amiss. Then Carlos frowned faintly, stopped and looked over his shoulder.

Peter was already out of sight. Carlos stood indecisively for a moment, his head tilted in thought. At last he took a pencil and notebook from his pocket, moistened the tip of the pencil with his tongue, and began to write an account of the incident.

Carlos was a meticulous policeman; he bored his superiors with extensive and accurate accounts of all happenings on his beat which seemed to him in any way curious or suspicious.

Carlos knew how his superiors felt toward him, but he had a notion they might not be bored with this particular report. Not if the rumors going around about the Banco de Bilbao turned out to be true.

Peter returned to his hotel room with a headful of worrisome considerations, none of which, however, was related to his plans for stealing the jewels and gems of the Virgins during the coming week. Cursing himself for a mooning, irrelevant ass, he flung his hat and coat in the general direction of a chair, and reached for the light switch.

He was troubled by guilt, troubled by innocence, troubled by the dubious purity of past and present motives; he was behaving as idiotically, as witlessly, as a man on a scaffold worrying about whether the drop would disturb the part in his hair.

Peter's hand froze on the light switch; he stood motionless, hardly breathing, while his remarkable senses scanned the dark and silent room for danger. Fool, he thought, irrelevant fool! Troubled by harmless thunder; ignoring the fatal lightning bolt.

76

He dipped a hand quickly into his pocket and took out a cigarette lighter. Gripping it tightly in his fist, he extended it at arms' length, parallel to the floor.

"*Ecoutez, mes amis,*" Peter said quietly. "Don't move; don't talk. I am holding three ounces of tri-nitrocellulose in my hand. Should I be forced to drop it—*Pouf! Et finis!*"

A gasp sounded behind Peter.

He snapped on the lights.

"Darling, what are you raving about?" Grace asked him anxiously.

5 ❧

"How DID YOU get in here?"

"I told the desk clerk I was a friend of yours. He said that made *us* friends, since you and he are friends. We all have passion, he said, and let me in. But please don't try to change the subject. Why were you going on that way in French?"

"As a matter of fact, I was expecting someone else."

"Yes. Tri-nitro whatever it was. *Pouf. Finis!* I guess you were." She smiled uncertainly. "Peter, what's wrong? You're different, somehow. You've changed."

And so had she, Peter realized sadly. He had always thought of her in images and metaphors. Silver trees, golden bonfires, stately clippers. Now in this transparent and cruelly realistic northern air, she seemed less mysterious, less a creature of magic and enchantment; she was human, after all, lovely beyond words to be sure, but weighable and measurable now, an entity composed of readily ascertainable details. She wore a dress the color of cocoa, a short coat of natural wool, and narrow black boots with tops of brown fur which fitted snugly about her fine ankles. There was a smudge of dust on her cheek. A tendril of fine hair had escaped a sleek coiffure to prance on top of her head like a tiny golden sea-horse. She must have come straight from the train, he thought with a pang of sympathy. She would probably love a bath and a nap. Somehow details he had never noticed before made her even more precious and dear in his eyes.

"Peter, you can't go ahead with this business," she said quietly.

"Dear, I've got to."

"But it's insane. It's worse. It's stupid and sentimental. When you told me about it at first, it sounded sweet and splendid. Like listening to a dear old uncle reading fairy tales before a cozy fire. But it won't work, Peter. There's no place for romantic gestures outside of books. I want you to be practical. To be sensible."

Yes, he thought, she was real enough now, no doubt of it. Sensible. Practical. But what had happened to the bonfires and cellos? Where had the enchantment gone? And yet, he thought, it probably wasn't her fault. It wasn't deliberate, at any rate. She must have been lulled to sleep, as he had been, by insidious and deceptive southern breezes. He remembered what Antonio,

79

the policeman, had told him about the north and south of Spain. It made a sad kind of sense now. The south sold gypsies and romance, ogres riding the west winds. While the north sold the things of the real world—good hotels and electricity, shops full of handbags and brass candlesticks. In the south, dreams of innocence and passion were understood and accepted as fancies borne on the African trades. But here in the north they were neither understood nor accepted; they were not sensible, not practical. But where, Peter wondered unhappily, did passion and innocence exist? In the needle of a compass? Or in the beat of a heart?

"Please listen to me, Peter. Please." He saw the tremor of her lips, the fear in her lovely eyes, and the way her hands were twisting together at her breast, and he thought wistfully of tall, silver trees, of stately clipper ships. How he missed them now!

"Yes?"

"I've got enough money for both of us. In twenty-four hours we could be halfway around the world. In Melbourne, Tokyo, or anywhere you like. Please come away with me, Peter."

"I can't. It just wouldn't work."

"Do you think this business will work? You're all alone, Peter. With no one to help you. You'll be caught and sent to prison, or you'll be shot and killed. Don't you realize that?"

"Yes, I suppose I do. But I can't help it."

"And I can't help caring about you. That's all I do care about, Peter."

"I wish my commitments were so simple," he said with a sigh.

"I am selfish and mean. You are loyal and pure. Is that what you're telling me?"

He said quietly: "You know I'm not taking a high moral stand. As you suggested, I'm trying to be practical. If I ran off with you and left my friends to hang, I'd hardly be the man you think you're in love with. I'm not sure who I'd be then. The change might even be an improvement. But you wouldn't have what you wanted, and neither would I. You'd have a nice sensible coward; and I'd have a woman who wanted a nice sensible coward. Neither of us would care for that. After a bit, we'd have difficulty looking at one another. Don't you see it wouldn't work?"

Unexpectedly she smiled and said, "Of course. You're absolutely right, Peter. You couldn't possibly come away with me. I see that now. So I'll have to stay with you. It's that simple."

"Don't talk like a fool!"

"But you've got no one else to trust. Your old friends aren't at your side. And Angela and Francois will sell you out the minute the job is done. They'll have to throw you to the police to protect themselves. Don't you realize that?"

"Of course. I'm not a complete idiot. But I'll have

something to say about that when the time comes."

"But you can't watch both of them. Please, Peter." She came closer to him and put her hands on his shoulders. There was a strange challenge in her smile, exciting lights in her splendid eyes. "Let me help you."

"Now you're talking like an idiot. You women pride yourselves on being realists. At bottom you're all as frivolous as tinkers." He pulled her hands down from his shoulders. He was quite angry. "This isn't a game we're playing. I'm not a knight in armor. I'm a thief. What I'm going to do—what I must do—is dangerous and wrong. Legally and morally. Will you get that into your silly head?"

"What's so immoral about it? What good are all those jewels doing strung about the necks of plaster statues?" There was a flash of mutinous tears in her eyes. "When families are cold and children are hungry? How can stealing them be morally wrong? You won't be depriving a single human being of comfort or solace."

He sighed. "That's very glib. If a man looks at a beautiful statue of the Virgin and says a prayer, who are we to measure what comfort and solace that may bring to him?"

"*I* can measure it. I would probably fit in a thimble, with lots of room left over."

"I'm not that omniscient, my dear." There was a touch of lofty admonition in his tone, and, sensing it, Peter resolved not to be presumptuous, regardless of

82

provocation. "I am a sinner," he continued more equably. "You are not. And I've never paid for my sins. That's the difference between us."

"Oh, how smug you are! It's the ultimate vanity, Peter, to accuse everyone else in the world of innocence. Because you equate it with naivety and stupidity."

"I'm sorry. But I do not."

"Yes you do. You think some special cachet attaches itself to sinners. While the mark of the booby is stamped on the innocent. Well, thank you very much, but I'm not a booby."

He was confused and stirred by her emotion, her closeness to him; the hot tears in her eyes melted the steel of his resolution. The drums and bugles were sounding once more; the tiny golden sea-horse on top of her head seemed to be prancing to the challenge of the music. He prayed for strength.

"Peter, please let me help you," she said, and as she whispered the words, the lights in the room coated her long full lips with a patina of shimmering silver.

"No, no, no!" he said. "The only way you can help is by leaving me alone."

She studied his face and eyes. Then she nodded and turned slowly to the door. "All right, Peter, I'll go, if that's what you want." She sighed and straightened her shoulders. "I have a confession to make. It doesn't matter in the least now, but I'm not pregnant."

"Oh? Is that all right? I mean, you're not disappointed or anything?"

She smiled quietly. "You're such a good man. Who else would think of such a thing now? It makes me feel rather small. Because I lied to you. I wasn't pregnant, darling."

"But you went to Paris and saw your husband. You said—"

She interrupted him. "No, I saw my lawyer. About some odds and ends of business. My husband's been dead four years. This is all very difficult, Peter. I told you he was alive and wanted me back because I didn't want you to feel responsible for me. If you wanted to throw me over, I didn't want you having conscience pangs about it." She sighed again. "You were upset about my children, and I realized I hadn't been fair to you. I wanted to give you, well—an out."

"I'm rather surprised at your estimate of me. Had I previously behaved in a fashion that led you to anticipate shrieks of prudish revulsion at what is, after all, a fairly natural condition?"

"You're spacing your words, Peter. You do it when you're upset."

"Damn it, why did you tell me this now?"

She turned quickly to him, her eyes bright with hope, "I thought it might make a difference. About helping you, I mean. I am, in fact, a perfectly proper widow with three adorably well-mannered children. I'm not a divorcee with shadowy ex-husbands and lovers. Don't you see the difference? It's such a perfect cover. I could come up here next week with my children and keep an eye on Francois and Angela. I could run errands for you, and help you with your plans. And no one would ever suspect me."

"God Almighty!" he cried explosively. "Didn't you hear me? Do you still think I'm trying to steal the plays of the Vassar volleyball team? You must be out of your mind! You want to help me?" He caught her shoulders and stared into her eyes. "All right. Find me cracksmen, dynamiters, human flies, judo experts. Get me Aristide Broualt! Christopher Page! Stuart Carmichael! Or Jimmy Fingers or even the Ace of Diamonds or the Count of Soho!"

"The Ace of Diamonds? The Count of Soho? What are you talking about?"

"You wouldn't understand if I spelled it out letter by letter. It doesn't matter. They are thieves. Geniuses, artists, virtuosos of crime. That's what I need. Not your proper widow's weeds and adorably well-mannered children."

"But they're all I have to offer you! How can you be so unfeeling?"

"It's not difficult at all, since it's my neck that's on the block." He picked up her purse and gloves and thrust them into her hands. "Now, will you do me two favors?"

"You're going to ask me to leave," she said miserably. "And you'll have the poor grace to consider that a favor. What else do you want, Peter?"

"I'd like you to say good-bye without rancor, without tears, without hysterics. And go out that door without looking back."

"You're so stubborn, Peter. You've made up your mind and nothing will change it. You can't think clearly any more."

"There is nothing left to think about," he said.

"If you weren't such a fool, you'd think about why I lied to you. And you'd wonder that I was able to. But you're not even curious. You're not only unfeeling and insensitive, you're rigid, and that's the worst possible drawback in your line of work."

"My work is running a bar. My cross is robbing banks. Will you please say good-bye now?"

"You're hateful."

Peter walked to the windows and stood with his back to her, his shoulders squared, arms folded, staring out at the winking lights of the old Basque town.

He was ready for this moment, quite ready for it. "Good-bye, Grace," he said quietly. But ready as he was, he was still surprised by the sharp edge of the words, surprised at the way they hurt his throat.

"Oh, good-bye, you bastard," she said.

Peter raised his eyebrows. That wasn't like her, he thought sadly.

86

He heard the doorknob turn; the hinges creak; the tap of her heels.

There was another sound then, a hiss of disturbed air that was like silk cloth being torn by angry hands. Something bright and shimmering flashed past Peter's startled eyes and impaled itself in the wall beside his head with a metallic *thunk*.

He ducked and wheeled about, but the door had already swung shut with a dry and final click. The room was empty; she was gone.

Peter stared at the slim little knife, which still quivered in the wall like a tuning fork. No, he thought, with some agitation, this wasn't like Grace at all. He worked the tip of the knife free from the plaster, and wondered what in heaven's name had got into her. Then his jaw dropped as he saw the playing card impaled to the hilt on the knife's gleaming blade.

The Ace of Diamonds. And on it a gryphon's head drawn in bold strokes.

The floor shifted giddily beneath Peter's feet. His mind turned an anagrammatical somersault, and the truth reverberated in his head with a crash.

The Ace of Diamonds with a gryphon!

The Grace of Diamonds!

The implications streaked through his mind like the shock waves of an earthquake. Grace! A criminal! Oh no, no. It wasn't possible. She was practical. Sensible. That was the reality; the bonfires had been an illusion, a chimera. Yes, that was it. It must be a joke. Of course. Laugh, you idiot, laugh. Ha, ha, ha!

Dear God, he thought, and rushed across the room and pulled open the door.

He collided with a tall man in a black raincoat.

"Excuse me, I was just going out," Peter said.

He stepped to one side, but the man moved quickly in front of him, blocking his way. Something hard and cold prodded Peter's stomach.

"Inside," the man said.

Peter glanced down and saw the shiny blue muzzle of a revolver. "Well, of course," he said, and stepped back into his room. The tall man looked down the corridor, nodding, and Peter took that opportunity to slip the knife and playing card into his pocket. Another man, with hard brown features and hair the color of old silver, joined the man in the black raincoat.

They came in and closed the door.

"Let me introduce myself," the older man said to Peter.

"That won't be necessary," Peter said. "You're Colonel Paul Brissard. He is Phillip Lemoins. I'm Peter Churchman and this is my room. So would you mind awfully telling me what this is all about?"

The colonel glanced at Phillip, then at Peter, his expression puzzled and suspicious. "You know who we are?"

"Yes. I spotted you a day or so ago. In a gray Citroen

cruising about everywhere I went. You might as well have sent up rockets. I tagged you back to your hotel yesterday afternoon, and the clerk told me who you were." Peter smiled. "But not why you're interested in me. Supposing you let me in on that."

The colonel shrugged lightly. "We're going to kill Francois Morel, Mr. Churchman."

"Bully for you! I wish you the best of luck."

"And you are going to help us, Mr. Churchman."

"I'm afraid that's out of the question. I've got quite enough demands on my time as it is."

"I'm not asking you. I'm telling you, Mr. Churchman.

"Oh? Then let me tell you to go to hell, Colonel."

Phillip struck Peter at the base of the skull with the muzzle of his gun.

"Speak in a civil manner to the colonel," he said, as he lowered Peter's sagging body into a chair.

"We aren't murderers in the usual sense, Mr. Churchman. We are executioners."

"Ah, yes," Peter said. His head ached. He was paying little attention to Colonel Brissard. His thoughts spun dizzily about Grace; the inside of his head was a cave of shimmering fantasies. Grace, in a picture hat and long white gloves, mixing explosives! No!

"Francois Morel isn't his name," the colonel said. "However, it will do as well as the one he dishonored.

89

Morel was a member of the OAS. So was I. And so was Phillip. Morel betrayed our general when things went badly. The details aren't important, but they may help you to understand us. Only one officer was allowed to know the whereabouts of the general's headquarters in Algiers. Morel and two accomplices tricked that officer into joining them at a house in the hills above the city. They overpowered him, bound him with ropes. Then they lowered the unfortunate man into a cesspool where rats fed. After twenty-four hours, with half his face eaten away, he told them what they wanted to know, Morel and his friends sold that information to the government to save their hides. Our general was captured and shot. In time we found Morel's accomplices. One was hiding in Aden, the other in Casablanca. We punished them with Biblical severity. An eye for an eye, isn't it, Mr. Churchman? We let rats feed on them until they died. It was disagreeable but so is treachery."

"The morality of this seems cloudy to me," Peter said. "You betrayed your country. Morel betrayed you. Where's the real difference?"

Phillip stood facing him, huge hands swinging free at his sides. The colonel now held the gun. "Speak civilly to the colonel," Phillip said gently.

"Never mind, Phillip. He's entitled to that question. Yes, we were rebels, Mr. Churchman. But it wasn't an easy decision. I knew St. Cyr as a youth. Verdun as a

90

young man. I served under marshals who lighted the sky like gods." He sighed faintly. "It takes considerable resolution to forget such memories. But as I watched the great forts of the empire falling one by one—not to arms but to political considerations—I joined a group that called such things monstrous. True, we lost faith in our leaders; but we kept faith with the glory of France. And now this is a paragraph of history, already blurred and obscured by the dust of time. But before the page is turned and the book closed forever, we will add a footnote concerning Francois Morel."

Peter asked what he considered to be reasonable questions. "Why not just go ahead and kill him? Why involve me in all this?"

"The woman Morel travels with is a thief. We know her reputation. We also know Morel got in touch with you several days ago. You met with Morel and his woman on at least three occasions. Then you came here to Pamplona. We assume you intend to steal something. We don't care what. You have our word, we won't touch your share of it."

"Now that's decent of you."

"Spare us your sarcasm, please. If you were a thief, that would be all that mattered to you. Money. But I don't think you're a thief. We made inquiries of you in the village. You've lived there six years, you own a business and so forth. So if I'm correct, you're being forced to cooperate. But not by Morel, obviously."

91

"Why 'obviously'?"

"Because we are familiar with his past, and we know his family, his friends and acquaintances. You didn't meet Morel until last week. Therefore it's the woman." The Colonel shrugged, certifying and dismissing this conclusion. "What we want is Morel's share of whatever you're planning to steal. Our general's family is living in poverty, and we feel it would be appropriate if Morel made a material restitution to them before he dies. If you refuse to help, we shall kill him immediately, of course." He smiled pleasantly. "Then, Mr. Churchman, what will the woman do when she learns that you allowed us to kill her lover?"

"But you intend to kill him, in any case."

"Ah, but she doesn't know that."

Peter damned the sly old logicians of St. Cyr; the colonel had built a neat trap for him.

"Well, I have no choice, it seems."

"That's right."

Peter straightened and looked thoughtfully at Phillip. "I might be able to use him, you know."

"Mr. Churchman, you had better understand one thing. You aren't using us. We are using you."

"Oh, it was just a matter of speaking," Peter said.

"Morel was in my regiment," the colonel said. "Therefore I must keep out of this. But he doesn't know Sergeant Lemoins. Until the matter is settled, Phillip will stay with you. Get used to that: he won't let you out of his sight."

"That could be awkward. How will it look to Morel if I return from Pamplona with a great Gallic shadow at my heels?"

"I think you can figure out some explanation, Mr. Churchman. Considering what's at stake."

"Oh, I intend to, believe me," Peter said.

He sighed and slipped a foot behind Phillip's ankle. Then he slammed his other foot into Phillip's knee, and the big Frenchman sat down abruptly, a cry of anger and surprise exploding from his throat. The sergeant was a formidable animal, Peter noted with clinical interest; his body seemed made of hard rubber and steel springs. He rolled onto his shoulders, doubled his legs up swiftly, then hurled himself forward, hobnailed boots lashing out at Peter's face.

Peter slipped from the chair barely in time to avoid a broken nose and smashed cheekbones. Crouching, he said sharply, "Colonel! For God's sake! The door!"

When the colonel wheeled about, Peter stood, and, with a thumb and forefinger, plucked the gun from his hand.

"Now, let's establish some realistic ground rules," he said, the gun swinging back and forth between the two Frenchmen, as evenly as the bar of a metronome. "You want to avenge dead comrades. I want to save live ones.

93

I don't give one damn about your old glories and be-trayals and defeats. Not one damn. I could shoot you both without turning a hair. Give me an excuse, and I will. Get up, Phillip. You look like an ass lying there with your boots in my chair."

"I'm sorry, Colonel," Phillip said, as he untangled himself and got to his feet.

"It was my fault, Phillip." The colonel looked thoughtfully at Peter, a bitter self-reproof in his hard features, a reluctant respect in his eyes. "I misjudged you, Mr. Churchman."

"Well, those things happen," Peter said. "Now then. I can do two things which will put an end to this non-sense. I can call the police and have you both locked up for breaking into my room; then I can call Morel and tell him you're on my trail. The next you know, he'd be in Brazil or Iceland or Timbuktu. But I'm not going to do either of those things, because I have a use for this big chap here. You can have your crack at Morel when my work is done. But not until. And not unless Phillip agrees to take orders from me as unhesitatingly as he would from you."

The colonel looked thoughtful. "May I have your word that you won't reveal Phillip's identity to Morel?"

"Yes, but only on the condition that you do nothing to Morel until I'm finished with him."

"You have my word."

"In that case, you have mine. Here. Put this away."

He gave the colonel his gun and turned to study Phillip with an appraising frown. "Stand up straight, Sergeant. Tell me. Are you as strong as you look?"

Phillip shrugged impassively. "I'm as strong as I need to be."

"Good. The job I have in mind is very demanding. Morel's not up to it, I'm sure. And I'll be busy with other things." Peter pulled a table from the wall and placed it between two straight-backed chairs. "Sit down, Phillip. Facing me. Are you familiar with arm-wrestling?"

The question brought a fleeting smile to Phillip's lips.

"Good," Peter said. "Let's see if you're up to what I have in mind."

They braced their elbows on the table and locked hands together deliberately and cautiously, adjusting and altering their grips for maximum power and leverage.

"Colonel, will you give us the word?"

"Very well. Are you both ready?"

"Yes."

"Yes, Colonel."

"In that case—commence!"

The table creaked with the sudden pressure of their arms.

The colonel smiled faintly. "Sergeant, put Mr. Churchman's hand down on the table."

"Yes, Colonel."

It was over in a matter of seconds.

Phillip rubbed his shoulder and looked sheepishly at the colonel. "I'm sorry, sir," he said with a sigh.

"Well, it's more a trick than anything else," Peter said, and gave Phillip a consoling pat on the back. "Don't worry about it. You'll do fine."

As Peter started to rise, Phillip sprang to his feet, stepped around the table and held his chair. There was something in his expression which brought a faint and rather wistful smile to the colonel's face.

"I hope I deserve your confidence, sir," Phillip said to Peter.

"I hope so too. For your sake and mine. Now let's discuss our problems realistically. It's all very well to say you want Morel's share of the loot. But getting it will be another matter. Angela is no fool. I'm assuming Morel isn't either."

"No. He has an instinct for survival," the colonel said.

"Therefore we need a sound cover story for Phillip. I am planning to steal certain precious stones from the Banco de Bilbao next week. But Phillip, you can't let on you know that. We mustn't get into the business of shares. Angela will question you, shrewdly and carefully, but you must convince her you think we're only after money. You don't know the details of the job. All you can reveal to either of them is this: that I offered you a sum of money, two thousand American dollars, to do something requiring great physical strength. It's dishonest, but you don't give a damn. Got it?"

Phillip nodded slowly. "They'll learn nothing more from me, I assure you."

"All right. Point two. When I hand over the jewels, I receive in return an object of no material value. Its nature isn't relevant. But it compromises friends of mine. Now let me say one more thing: The jewels have a sacred and historical value, and disposing of them may be impossible. I'm being fair with you—your general's wife probably won't realize a sou from them."

The colonel smiled. "If that's true—and we will make certain it is—we will return them to their owners."

"And kill Morel with pleasure," Phillip said.

"Then we understand one another."

"But I don't understand you," the colonel said. "You're risking your life—for nothing?"

The colonel smiled and turned to the door. With a hand on the knob he looked back at Peter. "You know, you're quite a remarkable person, Mr. Churchman. In another situation, I would like to be your friend. I think we might have interesting matters to talk about. But do you mind if I tell you something?"

"Please do."

"You have a disease which frequently attacked my finest officers."

"And what's that?"

"You want to die, Mr. Churchman."

The door clicked and they were gone.

The colonel's diagnosis jarred Peter. He didn't want to die. He wanted Grace, he wanted to live. What the devil did the old Frenchman know about it?

Troubled and unhappy, Peter went out to look for Grace.

He searched hotels and bars, cafés and restaurants, and looked for her shining blonde head in the streets and plazas of the old town. But he found no trace of her at all.

At last he gave up. He stood on the old battlements and stared down at the streets and buildings below him, and his mood was as gray as the soft gloomy dusk that was spreading over the city. Everything was quiet and peaceful now, but next week this would be the arena in which he must fight for his life.

Peter made his final preparations. He went to a crooked street where a carpenter lived and gave him money and instructions. Then he booked a hotel room with a view of the river and the bull pens. Finally he spent an hour in the reading room of the Museum of Archives, looking at blueprints of certain architecturally interesting buildings in the old quarter of the city. These precious yellowing documents, protected by sheathings of transparent plastic, gave Peter a scale view of the substructure of Pamplona. He made notes while the gently garrulous old curator explained the characteristics of the Roman sewers and canals which run under the older part of the town to drain into the river Argo. Peter drew the curator's attention to a particular building, and let him ramble on about it. He copied down a few more figures, thanked the old gentleman sincerely, and returned to his hotel room.

There he made an entry in his journal, a quite formal and explicit one: *Dear God. The others were for you. The passion, the innocence, the money, it was all for You. You look with favor, I'm told, on engineers who build bridges in Your Name, and on football coaches who win games for Your greater glory. Well, You know what I did. And why. But this one is strictly for me. Can I have just one for myself? Okay?*

There was no answer in the faint street noises drifting up to his room, no friendly encouragement or permission in the gentle stir of the curtains, the efficient drip of the faucet in the adjoining bathroom.

Well, no news is good news, Peter thought without cheer. He made himself a mild drink and began to pack.

6 ❧

ON THE MORNING of his return from Pamplona, Peter arranged a meeting with Angela and Francois at their hotel. He took Phillip along with him. At first Francois was as tense as a cat facing a mastiff. But after several cautious questions he relaxed and accepted Phillip with a relieved smile.

"So you weren't in Algeria at all?"

"No. My unit was in Lyons."

"You were lucky. In Algeria you never could tell who'd give you a knife in the back—the enemy or your own comrades. Of course, you knew about the revolts there, the OAS, that sort of thing?"

"Yes, but it wasn't my concern. I had a good job in the arms depot, and a reasonable commanding officer. Since I wasn't a professional soldier, it meant nothing to me that the generals in Algeria were squabbling among themselves."

Phillip was doing quite well, Peter decided; he sat with his huge hands folded in his lap, his eyes fixed neutrally on the shining sea beyond the terrace, composed and at ease.

Francois smiled at him. "They didn't fool you with their talk of glory and patriotism, I can see." He gave the big sergeant a friendly pat on the shoulder. "I'm glad to find you're intelligent. A man chooses well or badly, that's all there is to it. One choice makes a man a hero; the other makes him a traitor. Loyalty and honor are accidents since the verdict is delivered after the choice is made." Francois smiled at Peter. "You don't agree with me, I know. You believe in noble gestures. Loyalty to old comrades, regardless of risk or danger."

The glance that Phillip flicked at Francois' back was as swift and murderous as a flung knife. Peter noted it with alarm. He strolled past Phillip and gave him a small, warning headshake.

"Ah, you look troubled," Francois said complacently. "What does that mean? That you're not sure? That you have doubts about loyalty? About honor?"

"Francois, you bore me greatly."

"Oh? Is that so?"

"Yes. You have a rash of conscience, and you can't stop scratching it." Peter hoped desperately to create a climate of emotional turbulence; he didn't want to give Francois and Angela the opportunity to inspect Phillip with detachment. He didn't know whether Angela had spotted that revealing flare of anger in Phillip's eyes; she was reclining on the lounge, wearing a white bikini that was not much larger than the jeweled sunglasses which concealed her eyes. Peter couldn't tell what she was looking at, but he knew from experience that she was a precise judge of nuance and atmosphere.

"Peter, why are you trying to make Francoise angry?"

"I came here to discuss business. Not to listen to tiresome justifications of the rat act."

"But you're seldom so rude, darling."

"He feels he is indispensable," Francois said angrily. "We'll see how important he is when the job is over."

"What do you mean by that?"

"Francois, shut up! You too, Peter. Let's get down to work."

"Very well," Peter said. He had brought the films of San Fermin; the projector and screen were already in place. "Phillip, will you draw the drapes?"

"Yes, sir," said Phillip, springing to his feet.

The room became dark. Peter snapped on the machine. They all settled back and watched the flamboyant crowds in the Plaza de Castillo; the huge *Cabezudas* bobbing and turning high above them; fighting bulls tearing through the barricaded streets.

Peter froze the action at the square in front of the Ayuntamiento.

102

"Let me tell you what happens in Pamplona each morning of the fiesta," he said. "At the stroke of six a bomb is exploded near the river. That means the bulls have left the corral. When they form an *encierro* and start running, another bomb explodes. We will synchronize our blasting with those explosions."

Angela's eyes shone like a cat's in the darkness. "Oh, Peter, how clever you are!"

"Yes. The sound of our blasting will be completely drowned out by the roar of the bombs. We have twenty-six feet of stone and brick to get through. I estimate our progress at four feet a day; which means that on Sunday morning, the seventh and last day of the fiesta, we will reach the vaults of the bank." He walked to the screen and pointed to a passageway at one side of the square. "Now listen carefully. This leads to the basement of the warehouse adjoining the Banco de Bilbao. Each morning Francois and I will set off two charges in that basement. On the second one, the bulls will be running. Our job is to get back into the square, and clear out as fast as we can. We'll have about seventy seconds; we will need every one of them."

Francois swallowed with evident difficulty; the sound was quite harsh in the silence.

"Yes, Francois? What is it?"

"Good God! What about the bulls? They'll be on top of us."

"Yes, but that's the charm of it. The bulls are pure

gold, as far as we're concerned. Every eye will be on them. No one will notice us."

"But that's insane. Why not wait till they've gone by?"

"Because it won't work. The instant the bulls charge from the square, policemen and workers spring up. To handle the crowds and remove the barricades. We'd be spotted leaving the basement, or coming down the passageway."

"But what in God's name is to prevent our being gored? Or killed?"

"For my part I intend to run like the devil. If you think up anything cleverer, let me know. But, Francois, since my hide is just as vulnerable as yours, I've studied the possibilities very carefully. If our timing is precise, and no one panics, there's an excellent chance of bringing it off. Phillip, you can open the drapes now."

Sunlight splashed into the rooms. The white oval of the sea beyond the terrace was like the eye of a giant staring up at the sky.

"Now we come to your part, Angela. I want you to get up on Phillip's shoulders, and stand there till I tell you to get down."

"Are you serious?"

"Please do as I say. We have an enormous lot to do, and damn little time."

Phillip spread his legs wide, crouched slightly and gave Angela a hand. She put a foot against his thigh and swung up onto his shoulders, as easily and gracefully as if she were mounting a horse. Phillip cupped his hands behind her knees to brace her swaying figure. When he straightened to his full height, she gasped nervously.

"You're all right," Peter said. "Phillip, move about now. Skip and dance a bit." He glanced at his watch. "Let me know when you're tired."

"Very well, sir."

Angela shrieked as Phillip commenced to caper about the room with an air of elephantine gravity. She clutched at her bra and hissed questions at Peter.

"What's this for? What're you trying to prove?"

"Never mind. I'll explain later."

The telephone rang and Francois answered it.

"It's for you, Peter. Your barkeep, Mario."

Peter experienced a quick stir of hope and excitement. He had called Grace's villa three times this morning, but she hadn't been in. The maids had not been helpful; in fact, they seemed to have no clear idea of where she was, or when she might be back. All they knew was that she had not returned from Pamplona. This had added to Peter's confusion and apprehension. He was still shaken to the depths by the astounding implications of that slim little knife with the Ace of Diamonds attached to it. If it meant what he thought it did, how could he ever trust his judgment again? Or regard the world as anything but a crazy house of mirrors? But what else could that knife mean? He recalled the spiteful hiss as it whizzed past his ear. The metallic *thunk* as it struck the wall. And how it quivered there like a tuning fork, inches from his eyes. Had she tried to hit him? Or miss him? And where is she now? That was the most maddening thing of all.

He snatched the phone from Francois. "Mario? Did she call?"

"No, no. But Mr. Shahari is here. You said you wanted to talk to him."

"You're sure Grace didn't call?"

"Of course I'm sure."

He sighed. "Okay. Put Mr. Shahari on."

"Good morning, Mr. Churchman. What can I do for you today. Some money to change perhaps?"

"When are you returning to Gibraltar?"

"This afternoon."

"All right, I'd like you to do me a favor. I need a set of walkie-talkies. You can get them at Purdy's, I think.

"You wish me to buy them for you?"

"Yes. I'll be over to Gibraltar to pick them up tomorrow or the day after. I need a first-rate set, Mr. Shahari."

"The Japanese make a very good walkie-talkie. With a smart carrying case, imitation alligator leather."

"No. No Japanese. Zeiss or Audioflex. Don't economize, Mr. Shahari."

"Is there anything else?"

Peter hesitated. He didn't care to mention what else

he needed, not on an open telephone line. "Yes, there are several other items," he said. "But I think I'd better make a list of them. Can you wait in my office for a bit?"

"Of course. But perhaps you will do me a favor, Mr. Churchman. You know the fat American named Morgan?"

"Oh, yes."

"He tells people he is going to kill me in Pamplona. It had to do with his religion. Or philosophy. I'm not sure which. But it is very upsetting."

"I wouldn't worry too much, Mr. Shahari. I'll have a talk with him. Morgan's harmless. Last month he wanted to kill all the fishermen. He feels they're poisoning the world with iodine. Before that he tried to start a children's crusade to liberate Moscow. He thinks it belongs to Belgium."

"Belgium?" Mr. Shahari's voice rose slightly. "France may have a claim. But Belgium? He must be crazy."

"Yes. So stop worrying. If you'd like a coffee or brandy while you're waiting, just tell Mario. I'll be along shortly."

Peter put the phone down and turned his attention to Phillip and Angela. Tiny blisters of perspiration stood out on the Frenchman's forehead, but Angela seemed over her first queasiness and was now balancing herself with considerable skill.

"Well, Phillip, how do you feel?"

"I could go on for a while, sir. But there's an ache starting in my shoulders."

Peter glanced at his watch. This area of his timetable would be tight and chancy, too, he realized. He made a mental note to add Metrecal and Rye-Krisp to the list of things he needed from Gibraltar.

"All right, that will be enough. Come along, Phillip."

Angela slipped down from the Frenchman's shoulders and smiled at Peter. "It's too bad you have to rush away. But why not let Phillip stay with us for lunch? After all, we should get to know each other a bit better."

"I'm sorry, but we have work to do."

"Wouldn't you like to stay, Phillip?"

"Well, yes. But work is work, no?"

"Peter, don't you want us to know Phillip any better?"

She smiled but he noticed that she was drawing a fingernail slowly across the back of her small hand, plowing a thin white furrow in the deeply tanned skin. He couldn't bluff; she held the aces, of course.

He knew what she was up to. She wanted a line on Phillip, wanted to get her claws into him and scratch away at his secrets. But he realized it wouldn't be wise to refuse her a chance at him. That would only make her more curious. All he could hope was that the Sergeant was discreet and nimble.

Angela read his expression and smiled a victor's

smile. She hooked an arm companionably through Phillip's and looked up at him with innocently masked eyes. "We'll have a good talk, won't we? Francois, ask them to send up some wine. We'll order lunch later."

Peter went away with heavy misgivings.

Morgan had lost Quince. This had made him sad. On the sunny terrace of Peter's bar, he confided his gloom and disquietude to new friends. "Quince was a good chap, but he had his quirks like the rest of us. Had a fear of things getting around, as he put it. Well, turn down a glass. All we can do now. He's gone back to Wales. Didn't say why. He was a deep one, all right." Morgan smiled mysteriously and tapped his forehead. "But he had quirks. Afraid of things causing rows."

Morgan's heavy sigh caused a gentle ripple on the surface of his vast stomach. "Good old Quince. He needn't have worried about it. We could have killed Mr. Shahari quite easily. Taken his money, and thrown it about like confetti."

Until that instant, Morgan's grip on his audience had been very tentative; the two Americans who shared his table by accident had been idly watching girls saunter through the sun-splashed plaza; they had kept their interest in Morgan's nostalgic ramblings quite well in hand. But now they exchanged glances of mild curiosity. Then they shifted in their chairs and looked thoughtfully at Morgan. Their reactions seemed almost reflexive; they responded to the mention of money as men with hearty appetites might have to the sound of a steak beginning to sizzle in a frying pan.

Their names were Tonelli and Blake. Tonelli was the smaller and older of the pair, with thinning gray hair and the eyes and mouth of a migratory used-car salesman. He wore black slacks, a red sports shirt, a gold wrist watch and a "sportsman's" ring. Blake was a hairy man with bunched-up features and bunched-up shoulders. Tufts of hair grew from his ears. More of it, the color and texture of steel wool, sprouted from the collar of a wash-and-wear shirt, which seemed to have seen considerably more wearing than washing lately. Blake's eyes were muddy and dim, and his temper was chronically bad. He enjoyed pushing things to their ultimate limits, whether it was machines or animals or people, but that instant of fierce pleasure which accompanied the breaking point was so painfully fleeting that it set up all kinds of agitations and frustrations inside his head. Blake hated things that quit just when he got them going full speed.

Tonelli's practiced grin flickered over his lips. "Who'd you say you were planning to kill, Fatso?"

"The money changer from Gibraltar. Mr. Shahari. But he's a victim like the rest of us. Know who we should get our hands on?" Morgan peered warily at groups of incurious patrons seated near them, shifted closer to Blake and Tonelli, his great face rippling with secrets. "Got to get the lawyers," he said, lowering his voice. "They feed on people in trouble, right? And since everybody's in trouble, everybody's fair game, right? Look at you two poor devils. You're thieves, I imagine. In trouble, aren't you?"

Tonelli stared at the mountains and said quietly, "You got a big mouth, Fatso."

"You could catch something in it," Blake said.

Morgan looked pleased; he leaned forward, chuckling, and the press of his stomach drove the table into Tonelli's ribs.

"Of course you're thieves. You've been stealing God's precious air since the day you were born. Right?"

"Oh," Tonelli said, rubbing his side. After a moment of consideration, he added: "Well, if you look at it that way, you got a point, Fatso. But let's talk about this Indian, this Mr. Shahari, for a minute. He's got a lot of money, I guess."

"Oh, yes. One day he'll have it all. But he wouldn't come to Pamplona."

"What's that got to do with it?"

Morgan looked judicious. "Quince would be the man to see about that. He was a deep one, you know."

"Well, what were you going to do with the Indian's money?"

"We planned to scatter it about the city. A gesture of contempt, you understand."

Blake said wearily: "Let's find a bottle and go back to

the hotel. "Maybe we can get something besides a *muchissimo gracias* from them maids."

"No, not yet," Tonelli said. "Fatso's got me hooked. Okay, Fatso. The big question. Why wouldn't the Indian go to Pamplona?"

"Well, he can't. The government smiles on him in the south, but frowns on him in the north. He has a territory, you see."

Tonelli nodded slowly. "So if he got robbed up north, he couldn't squeal to the cops. That's interesting. Tell me something else. What made you think he'd go to Pamplona in the first place?"

"He would if there were enough money involved," Morgan said sadly. "He's very greedy. But he didn't trust me. You see, I told him I wanted to change twenty thousand dollars. I told him I got it from my father's estate."

"Your old man's dead?"

"No. That's why Mr. Shahari lost confidence in me, I think." Morgan sighed philosophically. "He's a stickler for detail."

"But let's say someone he trusted asked him to bring a lot of money to Pamplona. He'd do it, right?" Tonelli stared hard at Morgan. "Well? Wouldn't he?"

"Pay attention, Fatso," Blake said.

Morgan was smiling and waving at a red Porsche which had just pulled up before the terrace of the bar.

112

"Come over and have a drink, Peter," he called out happily. "I want you to meet my new friends."

"A pleasure," Peter said, nodding to the men who had been introduced to him as Mr. Blake and Mr. Tonelli. He summed them up with an experienced eye, and was not impressed by the totals. They looked tough and street-smart, and shady as a rainy day.

Peter smiled and patted Morgan on the shoulder. He liked Morgan. Morgan was quite easy to do business with. "You've been giving Mr. Shahari a bad time," he said.

"Oh, that's all over, Peter. Would you tell him, please? It's the lawyers we want to get our hands on."

"Well, he'll be relieved to hear it."

"Peter, are you going to Pamplona?"

"Yes."

"It's a blast, I hear," Tonelli said, grinning. "Bunch of nuts running around in front of cows. Booze, broads, the works." He winked at Blake. "We might give it a whirl, eh, old buddy?"

"Sure. What'd you think, Mr. Churchman? Think it's our kind of town?"

"You'll be perfectly at home," Peter said pleasantly. "Everything's on the American plan, even the jails." He gave them a nod to share between them and went on into his bar.

Tonelli looked after him. "Big deal," he said drily, and smiled at Blake.

"Big deal in a little game."

"Listen, Fatso," Tonelli said. "Does the Indian trust this character, Peter Whats-his-name?"

Morgan nodded enthusiastically. "Everybody trusts Peter."

Tonelli and Blake exchanged glances, and arrived at a meeting of minds. Tonelli put a hand on Morgan's arm. "Come on, Fatso. Let's go over to our hotel. We got some things to talk about."

"That's very kind of you. But I'm going to have lunch here. Why don't you join me?"

Blake put a big hand on Morgan's other arm. "Look, Porky, get used to doing what you're told."

They assisted Morgan from the table, and steered him into the street, maneuvering his great bulk through the eddying crowds like a pair of ruthless tugboats.

It was all very puzzling to Morgan. He would have liked to have a good talk with Quince about it. Quince would set him straight. No doubt of that.

In Peter's office Mr. Shahari sat neatly in a straight chair, his rings and fountain pens and gold teeth gleaming softly in the shafts of cool sunlight falling through the windows. With a polite and interested smile he read from Peter's list: "Diet chocolate and diet crackers. Yes. And six one-quarter inch chrome drills, specification

114

number two-nine-seven-eight. Ring-feed diamond cutter bar, Mark Seven. Trade name?" Mr. Shahari looked over his glasses at Peter. "I can't make it out, Mr. Churchman."

"The trade name is Wolverine."

"Oh, yes. Wolverine. And that's all?"

"Yes."

The Indian smiled benignly at Peter. "They will be expensive."

"I realize that."

"I have a friend in a sapper company on the Rock. A lance corporal who gambles unscientifically. I think he can find these items in their demolition stores."

"I'd rather counted on something like that."

"But there is a problem. Getting these items off the Rock may be difficult. If I were given to pessimism, I'd say it's quite impossible."

"I'll have to think about that."

"Yes. The customs officers are extremely sensitive to such items." Mr. Shahari smiled. "In the wrong hands, these tools might be put to criminal use."

"Yes, I see what you mean."

"Therefore, I must say one thing: While I may find these items for you, I cannot help smuggle them through customs. If there were any miscalculations, it would go very hard on me. And you, too, for that matter."

"You try to get the things I need. I'll try to get them off the Rock."

115

"I wish you the best of luck. It won't be easy, you know."

"Well, it's my headache, Mr. Shahari. Don't worry about it."

"In that case, I shall look forward to seeing you in Gibraltar. Perhaps you will let me give you lunch. I will ask my wife to make us a curry. Would you like that?"

"Very much indeed. And thank you."

"It's my pleasure, Mr. Churchman."

"You'll remember the walkie-talkies?"

"Yes, yes. Audioflex or Zeiss. No Japanese."

After the Indian had gone, Peter took a table on the terrace and considered his various problems. It was not an activity calculated to bring him peace of mind; there were dark clouds everywhere and not a silver lining in sight. Hawk-eyed customs officers at the Spanish border. Angela fishing craftily for Phillip's secrets. Lethal bulls pounding along barricaded streets. Twenty-six feet of stone and brick sealing off a great vault of tempered steel. And a timetable so exquisitely wrought that even a broken shoestring could smash it to bits. On top of all this there was Grace, flinging aside her mask to smile at him for being such a lugubrious fool. How amused she must be! But no. She hadn't been in a comic mood. Hurling that knife was not a light-hearted gesture.

The sun sank into the sea. Dancing shafts of lemon and purple light played over the softly molded flanks of

116

the hide-colored mountains. The air became cool. But still Peter sat frowning at his thoughts.

The life of the village flowed by him. The plaza was a busy hub, with streets stretching out like spokes to the markets, to the hills, to the beaches. Burros clip-clopped over the old stones. Maids in black uniforms with twists of jasmine in their hair hurried about on last-minute errands before the cocktail hour. Shoeshine boys and crippled lottery vendors screamed for custom-ers. A string of gypsies, complete from stooped ancients to black-eyed babies, stood out against the crowd like a tableau limning the ages of man. In their wake a tinker pushed a cumbersome wagon which was hung with dented and tarnished pots and pans. He was an old, old man with a flat nose and a beard the color of moss. At regular intervals he blew into a reed, and the sound rose and fell above the noise of the plaza in slow and mournful loops.

Peter straightened suddenly and stared at the tinker's rig with narrowing eyes. Ideas and schemes began to flicker in his mind like quicksilver. He noted that a can-opy protected the wagon from sun and rain. There was a workbench, a wooden tub of blackish water, a gas flame and soldering equipment, dull knives, sharp knives and broken knives, and a big stone grinding wheel connected to a sprocket and foot pedal.

Here was a link in the chain he must forge! Staring him straight in the face. He realized that he had been drifting listlessly toward swamps of despair and self-pity, ignoring the challenges he faced, doubting his own strength and skills. Enough of it, he thought, springing to his feet.

He hailed the tinker and went over to him. They talked for a few minutes. The old man named a price, which Peter slashed in half to indicate he meant business. After a series of proposals and counterproposals, each made in final and regretful tones, they struck a bargain which they sealed with smiling handshakes.

"You can depend on me, senor. Absolutely."

"I'm sure of it. Thank you very much."

Peter climbed into his car then and headed for the road which twisted up through the mountains to Grace's villa.

The Canadian girl who looked after the children let Peter in, but only confirmed what the maids had told him earlier; Grace wasn't at home, and no one seemed to know just where she was, or when she might be back. Peter felt quite deflated. He had been certain she was simply avoiding him.

A child in a white nightgown came into the living room and smiled tentatively at Peter. "Hello, Mr. Churchman. I thought it was Mommy, maybe. Do you still have that bad cat?"

"Why, hello, Debby."

"He made a mess on the floor," Debby explained to the Canadian girl. "The first time I went to Mr.

118

Churchman's house with Mommy. He's all black except for a spot on his chest. Would you like to come and see my sisters, Mr. Churchman?"

"Well, yes, of course. But maybe it's past their visiting hours."

"That's all right," the Canadian girl said. "They've had their supper and tubs. We usually read a while before bedtime, but I'm sure an unexpected visitor will compensate nicely for that."

"They're just babies, you know," Debby said. "Miss Marian, could Mr. Churchman read to them?"

"If he'd like to, yes, dear."

Debby smiled and took Peter's hand. "Come on. They'll fall right asleep. Then if you want I'll show you my flamenco dress. It's green and white. Mommy bought it and the maids sewed sequins on it."

They went down a wide and dimly-lighted corridor, with Debby pulling him along by the hand. She looked wonderfully sweet and well-cared for, like Grace in miniature, he thought sentimentally, with her scrubbed face and shining hair, and her eyes dancing with conspiratorial excitement. There were small blue flowers stitched about the high yoke of her white nightgown, and these, to Peter's eye, resembled the running lights of a ship, and heightened his illusion that her slender body was breasting the gloom of the hallway like a tiny graceful sail boat. Images, he thought anxiously. Was it something glandular in both mother and daughter that

119

prompted these metaphorical responses? When Debby stopped to look up at him, Peter fancied he saw sparks flashing in her eyes. Bonfires? No. But campfires, anyway.

She opened a door, and they went into an empty bedroom. There was a single lamp on a table, and drapes were drawn over the windows. Peter smiled at Debby.

"Well? Where are your sisters?"

"Bend down so I can whisper."

"Now what's this all about?"

Debby's lips brushed his ear, soft and light as feathers. "There's somebody sneaking around outside in the garden."

"Oh?" Peter glanced at the drawn drapes. "How do you know?"

"I was playing with Cathy and Elspeth in their room. After our baths. I saw him looking in our window. He was behind a bush."

"Did he realize you had seen him?"

"I don't know. He stood behind the bushes for a little while. I kept on playing like I didn't see him. Then he walked into the garden."

"Could it have been the gardener?"

"He goes home before dark."

Peter turned off the lamp and moved to the windows. Debby clutched his hand tightly. Peter drew the drapes back an inch or so, and let his eyes sweep over the gardens. In the darkness there was faint moonlight, faint breezes; trees and bushes were stirring gently, and the swimming pool at the foot of the garden shone like a patch of clouded silver. The gravelled walks gleamed in white irregular patterns where they circled lily ponds and cut through oleander hedges.

"Do you see anybody?" Debby whispered.

"No, everything looks normal." He let the drapes fall back into place and turned on the lamp. "Maybe you dozed off without knowing it, and had a bad dream."

"I wasn't dreaming. I saw him."

It must have been her imagination, Peter thought; she was indeed her mother's child, full of fancies and secrets. "Debby, why didn't you tell your nurse, Miss Marian, about this prowler?"

"Well, because she's so sensible," Debby said. "She's level-headed, and not afraid of anything. She's always laughing at the maids. She would have grabbed a flashlight and rushed right outside. That might not have been a good thing to do. But I couldn't have stopped her. That's why I told you."

Peter realized that her position was formidably logical. "You stay here," he said. "Leave the light on, but keep away from the window." He gave her a pat on the shoulder, and went swiftly out the door.

A car labored in the mountains. Fishermen sang in the straw-roofed bars on the dark beaches. Leaves rustled under slow, fragrant winds.

121

Peter listened intently to every faint sound, his senses scanning the garden like radar screens. Then he drifted along the wall toward the swimming pool. At the base of a lemon tree he found the stub of a Players cigarette. He squeezed the black tip between thumb and forefinger and found it still warm.

Clinging to the shadows, Peter crept about the pool, circled the bathhouse, and moved silently up a gravelled path that brought him back to the terrace of the villa.

He crouched in the shadow of an oleander bush, and peered through the green leaves and pink blossoms. He saw the lights in the living room where Miss Marian was reading and the lights in the bedroom where, hopefully, Debby was waiting for him. He could still hear the laboring engine of the car, and the singing from the beaches. But that was all. The silence bothered him; the garden was too quiet. Nesting birds and foraging insects were aware their domain had been invaded; tiny feathers and claws and feelers had all become still and motionless.

Suddenly—between him and the terrace—a footstep sounded on the gravelled walk. He froze. Silence settled again, and Peter knew that single revealing sound had been inadvertent; whoever had made it must now be crouching in the darkness, not daring to move, hardly daring to breathe. Peter took a rapid inventory of what he was wearing, and what he had in his pockets, but found nothing resembling a weapon. No penknife, no belt, not even a tie—

Again he heard a leather heel crunching softly on the gravel. After a few seconds the sound came again. . . .

Peter moved with infinite care about the curving bulk of the oleander bush, and saw the silhouette of a man in a dark suit standing only six or eight feet from him. He was staring up at the stone railing that rimmed the terrace.

Peter rose swiftly and silently through the darkness. "Put your hands up," he said, in a voice like a cracking whip. "Then freeze."

"Very well," the man said, in soft, musical tones, but even as he spoke he flung himself backward, swiftly as a cat, a foot lashing out murderously at Peter's groin. Peter dodged the blow and struck down at the man's back, his locked hands coming down like a savagely swung axe. He thought that would be the end of it, but the man's forearm swept about viciously and cut Peter's legs out from under him. They went to the ground in a churning heap, fighting for an advantage in the darkness. Peter struck with the edge of his palm, and was rewarded by a gasp of shock and pain. Then an elbow smashed into his jaw. He ducked another punch, locked an arm about a waist that was like whalebone, and, with a hip-roll, flipped the man into the oleander bush. With sweet and savage expectations, Peter leaped after him to finish the job, but a pair of feet slammed sicken-

123

ingly into his stomach, and he jackknifed, staggered, and fell into the murky waters of the lily pond.

Peter tried to get to his feet, but the man's weight landed abruptly and solidly on his back, as authoritative and unwelcome as an anchor. He bucked and heaved to get his head from the water and air into his lungs. His hands gathered fistfuls of lapels; he stood with a burst of strength, and snapped his shoulders down, catapulting the man over his head into the lilac hedge beside the pond. Peter splashed out of the water and leaped forward at exactly the right instant to catch a short, chopping blow on the chin that caused batteries of lights to explode before his eyes.

Lights were everywhere, flooding the garden.

Peter's patience was at an end; he swung hard and savagely, one, two, three times, and the sounds of his fists landing were like the sound of pile drivers slamming into hard-packed earth.

He jumped on his fallen foe, but the man laughed and struck him in the stomach with a blow that caused the air to burst from his lungs.

Peter got a grip on his throat and prepared to kill him.

"Stop it! Stop it, you fools!"

Dazed, stupefied, gasping for breath, Peter turned and stared blearily in the direction of that marvellously familiar voice.

The outdoor lights were shining, flooding the gardens

124

and the terrace.

They gleamed in Grace's eyes, gleamed in her golden hair, as she towered above him on the terrace like a splendid angry statue. At her side was a small round man with a bald head and shy eyes. Shock streaked through Peter like bolts of electricity.

He stared incredulously at the man he was sitting on, at the hawk-faced man he had been trying to kill; his head reeled; the tugs of reason strained at their moorings.

"No," he gasped weakly.

"I got here ahead of them, so I thought I'd take a look around. Lucky they arrived in time, eh?"

"Paddy, I might have killed you!"

"Ah, you old bastard," the Irishman said smiling. "It's good to see you, lad, even if you are choking the life out of me. Let me up now. This calls for stronger waters than you've got in that bloody fishpond."

Peter rolled off the Irishman and lay flat on his back, more spent and helpless than he had ever been in his life, while all the bright stars revolved about him in wild derisive circles.

"Let me give you a hand, lad."

"Easy now, you're all right," he heard Bendell say gently.

"Oh, darling, you do need a drink," said Grace.

Tenderly and gently, they took him up the stairs and into the villa.

7 ❧

THE SOUND of the engine trembled on the night air, diminishing and fading as the car followed the curving road down the mountains to the coastal highway. When the sound died away and only the wind stirred the silence, Peter sighed unhappily, for he felt very weary then, and very much alone.

"Oh, you're such a stubborn man," Grace said. "Worse than that, you're willful and selfish. You don't care a bit about your old friends. Or about me. How could you send them away, Peter?"

"Do you imagine it was easy?" He couldn't keep a trace of bitterness from his voice. "Don't you realize how much I'd like them with me? And how much I need them?"

Grace touched her eye with a handkerchief. "When I found Mr. Bendell in Liege, he was overjoyed at the chance to help you. But he felt you'd balk at using

126

Canalli. That's the only reason we didn't send for him. They didn't dream you'd turn them down, Peter."

It had not been easy, he thought sadly. He had told Bendell and the Irishman that there was no place for them in his plans, and they had had to take his word for it. But the Irishman, his eyes bright and hard as diamonds, had said, "Just one question, lad. Is the little bitch forcing you into this? Has that black-hearted harpy got something on you?"

"No, of course not."

"Peter!"

"Grace, keep out of this."

"What is it, lad? Give us a straight answer, for the love of Mary. Has that rotten, God-blasted bitch, Angela, got you where the hairs are short?"

"No."

Bendell had sighed and said: "Peter, my instincts tell me you are being noble."

"You should know me better than that."

"I do know you, Peter. I know you are generous and loyal beyond the boundaries of simple sanity. But as it was in the past, so it shall be now. You led and the rest of us followed. If you truly don't need us, Peter, we will go. Our presence here would only be dangerous to you."

"I truly don't need you, old friends."

They had sighed and raised their glasses to him in a last salute.

Now they were gone. Even the sound of the car had died away in the windy mountains.

Grace walked to the bar at the end of the long living room, and there was a suggestion of defiance in the decisive tap of her high heels on the cold marble floor. "I have a good notion to get drunk." She wore a black suede dress and black nylons, and her body seemed to merge with the shadows; in Peter's fancy, her bright face shone through the gloom like a glorious star mounted on a pedestal of exquisitely wrought ebony. "I should have told them the truth," she said, splashing whiskey recklessly into a cut-glass tumbler. "Yes. I should have told them about Angela and the film. And that you're risking your life to keep them safe and free."

"I'm very grateful you didn't."

"It was cruel not to. How do you imagine they'll feel when they learn the truth? When they pick up a newspaper one morning and find that you've been shot and killed? Or are in prison?"

"Damn it, they're not going to learn the truth. Stop worrying about me. I should think you'd have plenty to do just worrying about yourself?"

"What do you mean by that?"

Peter took the Ace of Diamonds from his pockets. It was quite soggy from his dunking in the lily pond; the gryphon's head was streaked and blurred almost beyond recognition. "Let's talk about you now," he said. "I became a thief for what may have been a ridiculous reason, but my motives were serious and honorable. What excuse did you have?"

"I didn't have any excuse. I didn't need one."

"There. That's something to worry about."

"Oh! What a moral snob you are! You look at me in disdain because I didn't have a nice, sentimental justification for stealing things. Supposing I told you I accidentally set off a landslide that wiped out a convent? And that I stole money so the nuns could rebuild it? Would that make you feel better?"

"Grace! Is that true?"

"Of course not, you silly man. I don't boast about what I did. But I don't apologize for it."

"Then you are simply an amoral criminal. I don't see anything cute or funny about that."

"I wish you wouldn't be so unhappy about it. Does it really mean that much to you?"

Peter slumped into a sofa and put his sodden shoes up on a coffee table. "Yes," he said gloomily. "It means everything."

Unexpectedly her mood changed; she smiled gently and tremulously, and sat beside him. She kissed his cheek and put her head against his shoulder. "Do you know why I love you so much? It's because you care about my soul. You'd like it to be as fair as my body, wouldn't you?" She turned her head and kissed the corner of his mouth. "As fresh and fragrant as a bowl of spring roses. I'd do anything to please you, Peter. But I can't do anything about my soul. I mean, I can't get at it with a pail and scrub brush. Would you like to hear the story of my life?"

"Would it be the truth?"

"I suppose you have a right to be beastly. I did lie to you once. But I won't now. My father died when I was a little girl. My mother remarried a few years later. He was a jolly little man with waxed mustaches and cheeks like apples. I loved him very much. Paul travelled a lot and when he came home he always brought me presents. Combs, mirrors, hairbows, boxes of candy, dresses with lots of petticoats. When I learned, much later, of course, that he was a thief, it didn't really make any difference to me. Paul never hurt anyone in his life. He would have fainted away at the notion of carrying a knife or a gun. And he only stole from the rich, of course."

"That's because the rich have the money. Robin Hood figured that out, too."

She smiled and tilted her head to one side. "Now you sound more like yourself, darling. Anyway, Paul got old and couldn't work, and we became poor. There were various uncles and aunts living with us by then, and the pinch was uncomfortable. It was very hard on Paul! He sat in the garden sighing over the past, and planning jobs just to keep busy, the way some people do cross-word puzzles. The plans were so clever it seemed a pity not to use them. So I used them. It seemed quite

130

normal, like carrying on the family business."

"So you all lived in luxury once again?"

"Well, we were comfortable at least."

"Grace, this is terrible. This flip, casual tone, this total lack of remorse, is ghastly."

She sighed. "I told you I couldn't do anything about my soul."

"All right then, why did you give it up?"

"It was because of Debby. When she was two-and-a-half or three, she told me she wanted to be a fireman. No, I'm quite serious. It made me think. You see, I had decided that there was something hereditary about what I did. Some compulsion that I wasn't responsible for. Naturally, I thought Debby and the other children would grow up with the same—well, proclivities. But here was Debby, a mere babe, striking out in a totally different direction."

Peter sighed with relief. "So you realized that what you were doing was wrong."

"No. I realized that stealing wasn't inevitable. I had enough money, so I gave it up."

"And you made no attempt to make amends? You have no remorse for what you did?"

"No. I guess not. Actually, I never thought about it very much." She put her hands on his cheeks, and turned his head to make him meet her eyes. "It's not important now, Peter," she said, softly and urgently. "All that matters is that you stay alive and stay free.

Please take me in your arms, and love me as I love you. And say you'll let me help you in Pamplona."

"No. Absolutely no."

"You think I'm not good enough. Is that it?"

"In a way you won't understand, yes."

"Oh you brute!" She leaped to her feet, hands clenching spasmodically, lambent sparks of anger flashing from her splendid eyes. It was marvelous to see; Peter was as entranced as if he were witnessing an electrical storm exploding over black, heaving seas.

"I'm sick of your lofty moralizing," she said furiously. "You patronize me because I was a common, ordinary thief. Because I didn't excuse my crimes by pretending I had some mystical partnership with God. Well, I'll show you, Peter Churchman. I may not have a lily-white soul, but I've got ten lily-white fingers that are just as clever as yours. If you won't let me help, I'll do the job on my own. And here's what you'll find when you open that vault in the Banco de Bilbao."

She plucked the Ace of Diamonds from his hand and waved it defiantly in his face. "Something to press in your souvenir book. My calling card."

Peter was shaken, not by her threats, but by her passion. With her slim strong legs spread wide, and the anger blazing purely in her eyes, she was like a creature struck from the ice and rock of mythology, proud, in domitable, fantastic.

132

"You are wonderful," he said simply. "Absolutely wonderful."

"Then why don't you let me help you?"

"I love you too much. And secondly, I don't need you."

"Oh, you are cruel. You melt my heart with one word and break it with the next."

And suddenly, for the first time since he had known her, there was weariness and defeat in the proud line of her shoulders. She turned quickly away, but not before he saw the bright flash of tears in her eyes. Peter wished desperately that he could find words that might give her some measure of hope or comfort, but he realized that anything he said would only ring with a hollow and hurtful banality. He turned to the door.

"Peter?"

"Yes?"

She looked steadily at him. "Will you promise me one thing?"

"Yes?"

"If you need me, if you really need me, will you promise to let me help you?"

The adverb she had used made it less difficult for him to lie; for he knew he could coat the word "really" with many slippery philosophical meanings. "Yes, you have my promise, dear."

Perhaps she believed him, perhaps she didn't; her

eyes and face, calm with hurt, told him nothing. He sighed and went away.

That night he wrote dejectedly in his journal: *To be indifferent to Divine Law is to put your faith in the practical; and see what a botch practical people always make of things. Grace must not be indifferent; she can't be.* After a moment of reflection, he addressed an irrelevant inquiry to the page: *Is Atheism really the best defense against Agnosticism?* Then his mood changed, and he wrote: *She is more philosophical about this mess than I am. I am censorious. (Moral snob?). While she is realistic. (Moral spastic?) Everything is suddenly turned around. Stay awake, dreamer, for things are not as they seem. Not ever.*

He re-read what he had written and tried to make sense of it. There was a kernel of truth hidden away somewhere, but he couldn't find it. All in all, he decided morosely, it wasn't one of his better efforts. Peter wished he were someone else, or someone different.

Thinking of it, he wrote: *In time of crisis the truly wise man panics; for the cool of head and stout of heart are always invited to repel attackers.*

Peter had a talk with Angela before he left for Gibraltar the following morning. Francois was not present.

"He's running on the beach," she explained with a slow, sweet smile. "Every morning and every afternoon, he runs on the beach. He's quit smoking, too. Do you imagine he's worried about the bulls?"

"I see how that possibility distresses you."

Angela's smile became silky. "Poor man. He's extremely sensitive to physical pain. Perhaps its because of things he saw and did in the war." She lay spread-eagled on a double lounge, immolating her slim body to the rising sun. White patches of gauze covered her eyes, but the soft, dreaming curve of her lips betrayed a sensual stir behind the delicate shell of her forehead. When she stretched her arms above her head, the rise of her ribs gracefully rounded the gleaming hollows between her small breasts and hips.

"Are you worried about the bulls, Peter?"

"I can handle my end of the job, I think."

"You were always so brave."

"But you're going to make a mess of yours."

"Oh?" She rolled onto her stomach and arranged herself comfortably. "Would you like to rub some cream on my back?"

"I didn't come here to do Francois' chores. Tell me this: do you have any intelligent plans for getting the jewels out of Spain?"

She smiled. "Francois has no zest for his chores since he began training. He eats yogurt and salt pills and vitamins, and sleeps at night on the sofa. But it isn't jewels, Peter; it's diamonds. You will take only diamonds. The Countess of Altamira's Net and Trident of

135

diamonds. The Diamond Flutes of Carlos. Nothing else."

"And have you thought of what will happen when they're found to be missing? Every customs point will close with a crash. A ring of guns and troops will circle the whole country."

"Yes, but with luck they'll be too late. You and Francois will have the diamonds on Sunday. The bank remains closed till Monday. By then—by Sunday night actually—the Flutes of Carlos and the Countess of Altamira's Net and Trident will have been flown from Spain under a diplomatic seal." She smiled and moved her feet slowly up and down like a swimmer. "We have another partner, Peter, a South African with the embassy in Madrid. He and Francois and I will be thousands of miles from Spain when the theft is discovered. The real trick is that the international diamond cartels will do anything to prevent these stones from reaching the market. There are collectors, of course, who wouldn't give a damn that they were stolen; in fact that might even add to their value in certain areas. And so everything's been arranged. You may set your mind at ease, Peter. Angela has her specialties, as you have yours."

She removed the white gauze patches from her eyes and looked at him without noticeable friendliness. "But my future plans don't concern you. I just want you to realize I'll be comfortable. Thinking of that should amuse you. Now let's talk about that great ox, Phillip. I don't like him, I don't trust him."

"Why not?"

"Because there's something cold and cruel in his hands. When he helps me from his shoulders I feel that he'd enjoy snapping my spine like a celery stalk. And when he thinks no one is watching, he stares at Francois in a strange fashion. As if he despises him."

"You can't blame Phillip for sharing a majority view."

"How did you meet him?"

"I've explained that."

"Then explain it again."

Her mood was getting worse, he saw. He shrugged. "I got talking with him in Pamplona. I saw he had the three things I wanted: greed, physical strength, and a lack of imagination."

"I want you to get rid of him."

He shook his head. "Either I run things, or I don't. Make up your mind."

"All right," she said slowly. She sat up and regarded him with an appraising smile. "I really don't like you, Peter. Do you realize that?"

"Yes, and it grieves me keenly. Now let's talk about the film, shall we? I want it the morning Francois and I enter the bank. Francois will bring it along with him. Otherwise, I won't blow the vault. Do you understand?"

"What makes you think you can give me ultimatums?"

"Because, Angela, I don't like you either. And the tensile strength of my bondage isn't infinite; you'd be wise not to strain it."

"Peter! What would I gain by double-crossing you?"

"Why nothing, of course." He smiled into the shimmering lights of her narrowing eyes. "I've sent Phillip on to Pamplona. I suggest you and Francois leave tomorrow. We're almost at the point of no return now. So remember my terms: no film, no diamonds."

She smiled back at him and nodded slowly.

Peter rose to leave. The crucial information he took away with him was that their trust and confidence in one another was nonexistent. If faith could move mountains, theirs wouldn't budge a feather.

At Gibraltar British destroyers cruised over the green waters between Spain and Africa; the broad white tail of the tourist ferry was hull-down on its way to Tangier; whistles blasted the mild air, and gulls flew about with an expertise that seemed tinged with panic; fishermen with brandy and cheap watches and hashish in their boats rowed steadily but cautiously toward a Dutch freighter anchored in the Straits, while on the Rock itself, Indians and Tommies and Spaniards mingled in the streets, and children played cricket in squares ringed with venerable cannons.

Mr. Shahari's shop was in the High Street. Bright

silken kimonos and black lace negligees fluttered over the sidewalk, offering splintered glimpses of merchandise piled up behind dusty glass windows. For tourists and seamen there were Swiss watches, Toledo blades, watered perfumes, cuckoo clocks, banderillas in red and white streamers, figures of the Virgin and the Buddha, jade necklaces and bracelets, tambourines, castanets, guitars, and gaudy scarves emblazoned with the images of Roy Rogers and Gary Cooper, of stallions muzzling mares in front of Canadian sunsets, of the peerless Manolete gazing sorrowfully at idealized bulls and senoritas.

As Peter hurried toward this cornucopia of frivolities, he ran into Cathy Clark.

"Oh, Peter, how lucky. I'm so worried. I've got to talk to you about Morgan."

At sight of her, Peter's soul had curdled like an oyster dropped in boiling milk. That reaction was hardly fair, he realized; Cathy was young and innocent, and her voice was not at all like most Americans, but still, she had been in his office when he had received the summons from Angela—how many decades ago had *that* been?—and her presence recalled the shock of that moment all too vividly.

"I'm very rushed."

"But Morgan's in terrible shape, Peter. I went to see him yesterday. He's going up to Pamplona with those ghastly Americans. Do you know them? One is so hairy he sheds. He really does. And the other one, his name's Tonelli, I think, he looks like, well, like he'd love giving a multiple hotfoot to a centipede. Have you met them?"

"Yes."

"They're so cruel to him. They call him Fatso and Porky. And he doesn't rant and rave like he used to, he just sits there and heaves big sighs. Are you a lawyer, Peter?"

"What gave you that idea?"

"Morgan seems to think you are. Peter, he's in trouble. I know it. Can't you do something about him?"

"Well, what do you suggest?"

She frowned uncertainly. "I don't know. But those men have a hold on him. He shouldn't go to Pamplona with them."

"Cathy, if Morgan wants to go to Pamplona, I can't stop him. I'm late now. Excuse me."

In the small office behind his shop, Mr. Shahari smiled complacently at heaps of merchandise on his desk. "I believe it's all here, Mr. Churchman. The diet crackers and diet chocolate. The walkie-talkies, everything."

Peter inspected the walkie-talkies, and placed them in his attaché case, along with the crackers and cans of milk.

"There will be no trouble with those items," Mr. Shahari said. "In fact, it will please the Spanish customs officials to find a wealthy man who must nourish

140

himself on dry crackers and milk that tastes like chalk. It will make them pleased with the prospect of the chickens and rice and wines that are waiting for them in their own homes. But as for the other things—" he looked soberly at the shining heap of precision tools on his desk . . . "they are another matter altogether."

The bits and braces and drills sparkled palely in the light of the single bulb hanging from the ceiling. They looked powerful and cruel, like ferocious metallic animals, with deadly little jaws, savage claws, rows of glistening pointed teeth. They actually looked hungry, Peter thought, as if they were eager to start tearing and champing at a banquet of bolts and hinges and locks.

"You will need luck," Mr. Shahari said.

"I know."

"In fact, you'll need a miracle."

From the alley behind Mr. Shahari's shop came the sound of low and mournful piping. Peter looked at his watch.

"Maybe there's my miracle."

Mr. Shahari raised his eyebrows. "No, Mr. Churchman. That is only a knife sharpener."

Peter opened the back door of the shop. The old tinker with the mossy cheeks stood beside his wagon in the alley.

"You see, I told you that you could depend on me," he said. The old man seemed in high spirits; his smile was wide, and his eyes gleamed with conspiratorial excitement. "We'll play a good trick on them, eh senor?" There was a wine bottle in his pocket.

Peter collected the drills and braces and carried them to the doorway. After a glance up and down the alley, he went outside and spread the tools on the work surface of the tinker's wagon. The old man smeared them all with thick coatings of black grease and, one by one, dropped them into the wooden tub of dirty water lashed to the side of his rig. On top of them he threw a half-dozen broken knives, and several dented pots and pans. When they disappeared from sight, he pantomimed smoothing the surface of the water with his hands, as if he were tucking them all away in bed. This set him to laughing hugely. Overcome, he clutched his sides, and turned a flushed and merry face to Peter.

"What a trick," he cried, between gasps. "What a trick!

"Yes," Peter said, a bit nervously, and glanced at his watch. "Now you must reach Spanish customs at exactly four-thirty. Before the day laborers check out. Got that?"

"You can depend on me," the old tinker said, and, still laughing heartily, he trundled his wagon off down the alley.

"It's very clever," Mr. Shahari said. "I wish you luck, Mr. Churchman. Now, would you care to glance at this bill?"

Peter lunched late at the Queens. He had a fine meal.

Prawns, *paella*, lamb chops, and assorted cheeses, which he funneled down with the aid of a half bottle of Banda Azul and several brandies. Then, as the sun and his spirits began to sink, each inevitably and irrevocably, he paid the check and went off to collect his car.

The standards and guidons of historic regiments sang in the breezes above the ramparts of the Rock. On a cricket pitch near O'Hara's Battery, a sergeant-major shattered the air with furious roars at a platoon of drilling soldiers.

Peter drove with outward composure past landmarks whose names rang with the march of empire; the Bastion of Orange, Ragged Staff, and St. Jago's Barracks— but his thoughts were not of cavalry charges and riotous natives, but of the customs officers a mile or so ahead, with their neat uniforms and white gloves and X-ray eyes.

The barriers were down at the air field. He waited for a BEA jet to come in and land, then drove across the runway and joined the tail-end of a queue of cars and trucks waiting to be checked through into Spain. In another line were laborers, burros, horse-drawn wagons, tradesmen pushing handcarts.

The two lines came together as they neared the customs point. Peter cut his engine and studied the officers who were examining luggage and parcels in the cars ahead of him. Sometimes it was possible to sense their mood and to guess at the probable intensity of their inspection. On occasion this amounted to a smile and a casual wave in the direction of Spain. But today things looked serious. Tourists were being sent with their luggage into the offices that adjoined the checkpoint. Laborers were emptying rucksacks onto the ground. White-gloved hands poked into burlap bags slung over burros, delved into suitcases and valises, fingered and threaded their way through the contents of bundles and blanket rolls.

Peter spotted his tinker in the line opposite him. The old man was advancing on the customs point in noisy stops and starts; when he braked his wagon the pots and pans hanging above the work bench banged together like cymbals; when he shoved it forward they set up another tinny clamor, and the water in the wooden tub sloshed over the sides and made black patches in the yellow earth.

The old man saw Peter and smiled widely at him. They were abreast of one another now, not ten feet apart. The tinker waved at Peter. Peter looked away. He could feel his heart pounding.

"Senor! Senor!"

Peter gave him a fleeting smile to quiet him. The old man chuckled, and winked at him.

An officer came over to Peter's car.

"You have any firearms? Whiskey? Cigarettes?"

"No, I don't."

"The old man knows you, eh? Please open your brief case.

144

"Yes, he came up to my villa last week to sharpen the knives. He's a good man. Very honest and industrious."

"The brief case, please."

"Yes, yes, of course."

Another officer was inspecting the tinker's wagon, peering into pots and pans, gingerly picking over a tray full of dull and broken knives.

"These crackers and cans of milk? They are for your children?"

"No, they're for me."

The officer looked at him skeptically.

"You like such food?"

"Well, it's not a question of liking it. I'm trying to lose some weight, you see."

The officer shrugged. "We will lose it all when we die. Why hurry?" He examined the walkie-talkies with more interest. "And these? They are radios?"

Peter explained their use, and the officer copied down their serial numbers.

"Have a good trip, senor."

"Thank you very much."

In the opposite line the tinker grinned slyly at Peter. The officer who had been looking over his wagon was apparently satisfied. He stepped back and waved the old man on to Spain.

Peter slowly let out his breath. In the ultimate analysis, he thought, everything hung always on slender threads of chance; one could try to anticipate all eventualities, erect the stoutest possible barricades against

145

the unforeseen or unexpected, and be prepared for any conceivable fall of the dice—and all to no avail.

For there were strains one couldn't predict, stresses one couldn't imagine. And these had a maddening way of adding their weight to considerations at precisely the wrong moment, at exactly the moment, in fact, when the gossamer threads of chance were already stretched to the breaking point.

Fate had an inexhaustible supply of booby traps, an infinite variety of sneak punches. She (or was it he?) was always waiting to let you have one in the groin or behind the ear. Cleverness was only half of it; you had to be lucky.

But now Peter's luck seemed to be holding strong. The tinker was on his way, pushing past the customs officer, with all his pots and pans banging a cheerful farewell to the Rock.

Peter said a silent prayer and started his car.

And it was then that all the threads of chance began to snap!

A jet flew over screaming like a banshee. Dogs raced away from the noise in mindless circles, eyes rolling, ears flat. The jet banked and a gust of wind intensified the squeal and hiss of ruptured air. A burro brayed deafeningly, broke away from his master, lashed out with his heels at anyone who came near him. He backed up to the tinker's wagon, kicking at it savagely, and one of his bony, rock-hard hooves splintered a stave in the wooden tub bolted to the side of the rig.

Peter watched in horror as water began to trickle from the cracked tub; he could not have been more dismayed if his own life's blood were spilling out on the ground at the custom officer's feet.

The level of water in the tub dropped slowly and steadily, revealing pots and pans at first, then an assortment of knives, and finally the grease-smeared tools he had acquired from Mr. Shahari.

The customs officer looked at them with a frown, more puzzled, it seemed, than suspicious. Peter silently cursed the old tinker, who stood frozen with apprehension, a weak and guilty grin flickering through his mossy beard. Move! Go! He tried desperately to catch his eye, but the tinker was staring at the customs officer like a child caught with his hand in a cookie jar.

Slowly, and with an air of surgical fastidiousness, the officer drew off his immaculate gloves and tucked them under his belt. He had not quite reached a decision, he was not thoroughly committed, Peter realized with a flare of hope; his ferretlike instincts had not yet caught a whiff of quarry. He shrugged and glanced at one of his incurious colleagues, inviting the officer's attention to the dully glittering objects in the wooden tub. The second officer frowned and strolled over to the wagon, pulling off his gloves.

Peter sighed and raised his eyes to heaven.

A sudden, accelerating roar sounded behind him; and

Peter gasped as he flicked a glance at his rear-vision mirror.

"No!" he shouted, vainly and fruitlessly, and threw himself to one side.

There was a bucking, sickening crash. The impact flung him against the dashboard, and he collapsed to the floor as batteries of brilliant lights exploded painfully inside his head.

Dimly he heard squalls of agitation and confusion howling outside his car. There were shouts, screams, brayings, barkings. Someone jerked open the door that partially supported his weight, and Peter fell out of his car onto the concrete ramp of the customs point.

A voice said tearfully: "I must have stepped on the accelerator instead of the brake. I'm so terribly sorry."

"Are you hurt, senora?"

"No, no. But I deserve to be. The fool that causes the trouble always gets off without a scratch."

"You're too hard on yourself, senora. Machinery isn't infallible. It makes mistakes, too."

Another solicitious spanish voice said: "I believe you've bruised your knee, senora."

"It's nothing. Oh, please see if he's hurt."

Peter raised his cheek from the cold and oily concrete, and blinked in confusion.

Grace stood encircled by a cluster of sympathetic customs officers, dabbing at the pretty tears sparkling in her eyes. One of the men whipped an immaculate handkerchief from his tunic and applied it delicately to the scratch on her knee.

Another officer waved impatiently at the line of laborers.

"Look, move along. There's no need to gape and stare. Old man! Get your wagon moving. You've been cleared, haven't you?"

"*Si, si, si,* senor."

Grace sank down beside Peter. "Are you all right, sir?"

Peter watched the old tinker trundling his wagon into Spain, knees and elbows pumping like pistons. The rattle of pots and pans was soft and sweet in the mild air.

"I'm fine," Peter said with a sigh.

Grace put a hand gently but tentatively on his arm, "May I help you? Please?"

There were forms to fill out, statements to sign and Peter's car to be towed back to the garage on the Rock. Grace's Bentley, however, was not seriously damaged. She offered Peter a ride, and this gesture pleased the customs officers. They smiled approvingly, their hearts and fancies quickened by the sweet and logical fashion in which the Lord provided Samaritans with victims to look after.

Waving and smiling, they watched the Bentley roll on to Spain.

In the car Grace said quietly: "Are you angry with me?"

"I'd be a fool if I were. What did you do? Go to Mr. Shahari?"

"Yes."

"He told you what I was up to?"

"Oh, no. But there was a bill on his desk with your name on it. I can read things upside down quite well. Can you?"

"Yes."

"Well then, I knew what you were trying to do." She smiled nervously. "You didn't answer my question, Peter. May I help you?"

He sighed. This was what she wanted, what she relished, what her soul was cut and shaped for; why should he cavil at using her, any more than he would hesitate to use the deadly and functional tools he had acquired from Mr. Shahari?

"On one condition," he said quietly. "That you do exactly as I tell you. Will you promise me that?"

"Yes, I will, Peter."

"Very well then. Listen."

8 ⤸

PETER STARED intently at the shining tips of massive horns. The horns swung searchingly from side to side, sunlight dancing on their black and ivory shadings.

"Toro?" Peter cleared his throat. "Toro?"

"No, no, no, Peter. You sound as if you're coaxing a kitten to take its milk." Don Miguel stamped a booted foot on the ground. "*Toro! Huh! Toro!* Like that, Peter. *Toro.* You don't crook your finger and say, 'Nice Toro, come here, little Toro.'"

Peter stood on hard-packed sand in the middle of the bullring at Malaga, holding a heart-shaped, heart-colored piece of flannel in his hands, and facing sleek, murderous horns mounted on the front of a wheelbarrow.

"Try again," Don Miguel said, nodding at the boy who stood by the wheelbarrow. "And Peter. Don't jerk

151

the *muleta* away from the horns. Think of a sail going taut on a long jib. Filling slowly and powerfully. Think of your wrists as that jib, holding and controlling the *muleta* as it swells with the horns of the bull."

"Well, yes," Peter said.

The circular stone tiers in the plaza were empty. It was a hot and dusty morning, and the sun on the yellow sand hurt his eyes. Perspiration blistered his forehead, and his shirt was plastered damply to his back and shoulders.

The youngster raised the handles of the wheelbarrow and waggled the big horns at Peter.

"Toro!" Peter said. Then he said, "Ouch."

"Rest a minute." Don Miguel stood against the *barrerra*, a smiling old man with hair that was still black, and eyes that were bright as live coals in his lean, tough face. His features were coarse and weathered, as if they had been hacked from a rock that had faced the storms of the world from a mountain top. Don Miguel, who was still called the Sword of Malaga by the press, wore a black suit, a wide-brimmed, flat-crowned gray hat, and brown leather boots. Around his neck hung a goatskin of wine. In his mouth was a thin, green-flecked cigar.

He unslung the *bota* and offered it to Peter.

"Take it. You need it."

"Thank you."

Peter raised the goatskin above his head, opened his

152

mouth, and pressed the bag until the air was gone from it and a jet of purple wine shot out and struck the back of his dry throat with a satisfying *splat*. He swallowed three mouthfuls of wine and handed the *bota* to Don Miguel.

The old man said, "Peter, there is eternal springtime in your heart, of course. But the green days and warm nights were bought by the silver at your temples." He regarded Peter with kindly amusement. "This is nonsense. Why do you want to know about the bulls?"

"I'm going to Pamplona tomorrow."

"Ah, and you want to run in front of the bulls during the fiesta?"

"That's it."

"Well, why didn't you tell me? It's the simplest thing in the world. You don't need to bother with the cape and *muleta*. In any event, Peter, you'd be arrested if you tried to use them in the streets. It's against the law. The bulls learn too quickly. But listen, what you do is this: Find a place in the front of the crowd. Take to your heels when you hear the first bomb. You can't stop for a nap, but if you run fast you'll be safe in the bull-ring well before the bulls."

"Don Miguel, I intend to run with the *suicideros*."

"Then you must be crazy."

"I can't explain. But I must do it."

"You mean once?"

"No, every day."

"Your troubles are so great that death is preferable?"

"No. Running will keep me alive."

Don Miguel looked at him thoughtfully. "We had better be more serious then. Listen, and I'll tell some things you probably already know. The trick is to remember them when you're facing a bull. When they run with the oxen, they aren't dangerous. As bullfighters say, they are on tracks." Don Miguel smiled, "Tales of youthful bravado are a bore, I realize. The bulls become larger with every year that passes. But let me tell you what we used to do at San Fermin. To start with, we drank all night. At dawn we managed it in one fashion or another to reach the Estefeta. Maids from our villas spread linen tablecloths in the street, set out china and plate, and served our breakfast. But not coffee and bread and butter! It was a feast. *Cocida*, roast pigs, *porrons* of wine. You know the *porrons?* They're like this goatskin, only made of glass. You tip them up and open your mouth and swallow until you can't hold any more. Well then we sat in the streets and ate and drank. The bombs would sound and the bulls would start running. But we continued eating and drinking. We never moved." The old man laughed. "There are pictures of this in my villa, I'm not making it up. We sat in the street and let the bulls run over us. Some of us were knocked over, but the bulls seemed glad to get away from us. Maybe they knew we were crazy. That is what it's like when they run with oxen."

He drank more wine. Peter did too.

"But a bull alone is different, Peter. Remember this. Sometimes a bull will trip and fall. The *encierro* pounds away down the streets. And the bull that is left alone now looks for something to kill. If this happens, you must stand still. If you move, he will charge. He may charge anyway, of course. Listen. I remember when bull-breeders gave banquets in their private bullrings. We sat at a long table in the middle of the arena. After many courses and many bottles of wine, a trumpet would sound, the *toril* gate would swing open, and out would trot an uninvited guest." Don Miguel smiled nostalgically. "Yes, a fighting bull. It was good to be quite drunk, then, or to have been born without nerves. The bull would circle the table, looking and waiting for someone to move. It was very difficult to hold a glass an inch from your lips and stare at his horns. And do you know what happened to the first man who lost his nerve and bolted for the *barrerra?*"

"No."

Don Miguel laughed heartily. "He had to pay for the banquet. Yes, he had to pay for everything. When are you leaving for Pamplona?"

"Tomorrow morning."

"Go with God, my friend. He will take care of you. If I were younger . . ." Don Miguel's voice trailed off. He looked thoughtfully at the tips of his boots. "Of course, God, Himself, is hardly a child any more."

"What do you mean?"

Don Miguel smiled warmly and gave Peter a pat on the shoulder. "It was nothing, my friend. Nothing but the irreverent rambling of an old man. Good-bye, Peter."

That evening Peter completed the last of his preparations. He stopped at the offices of the Terremoto Construction Company in Malaga and told them (truthfully enough) that he would like to open up a cove for small shipping on a piece of property he owned on the coast of north Algeciras. He needed dynamite; plungers and wire; dynamite caps. After a discussion of the technical aspects of the problem—and a glass of Anis— Peter drove off with the things he needed in the trunk of the car he had rented from the garage in Gibraltar.

The sun was dropping swiftly into a pale green sea. Pink and lemon lights coated the mountain peaks, but the road was already dark, and the fields of sugar cane that stretched away on either side of it seemed without detail or texture, as smooth as softly swelling waves.

Peter experienced a sense of resignation that was like a false peace. The outcome of this adventure was out of his control now, for in spite of all that human nerve and resolution might accomplish, success or failure was dependent on the whimsical threads of chance. His plans were masterful and sound; but one error, one miscalculation, one bad break, and they would all crash fatally about their heads.

That night he wrote decisively in his journal: *"Worry about the real, the weighable, the measurable world: your life, the life of your friends. To hell with her soul.*

The consignment was inadvertent. Oh no, he thought unhappily. No. . . .

Antonio Gonzalez y Najera, the policeman of the village, hailed Peter in front of his bar the following morning. Peter was busy loading a suitcase into the trunk of his car.

"Good morning, Peter. Off to Pamplona, eh?"

"Yes, Antonio."

The policeman smiled and rocked on his stout boots.

"Peter, I have some strange news. The police in Pamplona are suspicious of you. They called to make inquiries last night."

Peter was bent over, his head hidden from view by the lid of the trunk. He tried to straighten up, but couldn't; shock streaked through his body in rhythmic, paralyzing bursts.

"Yes, the chief of municipal security called in person. Peter. Imagine! My wife answered and very nearly fell over in a faint. Are you all right, Peter? Are you stuck?"

"No, no. It's just a twinge in my back."

Peter managed to stand erect, and, with considerably more difficulty, managed a mildly puzzled smile.

"You were discovered prowling about the rear of a

157

building adjoining the Banco de Bilbao, Peter. The policeman reported the incident to his superiors."

Peter laughed, a sincere laugh. He didn't need to fake it; his laughter was genuine and honest, for this was too calamitous a pratfall to take seriously. It was like the playful kitten battling loose the electric socket attached to an iron lung . . . the eager sprinter shot dead by the starter's gun . . . the skis falling off at the proud arc of the jump . . .

At such hotfoots of Fate, you could only laugh until you wept. . . .

"The policeman had an accurate description of you, Peter. Since there were few tourists in town, the police were able to check the hotels and find out who you were and where you lived. This took a day or so. Then they called me." The policeman's eyes twinkled. "To inquire of your habits and character. You can't blame them. They must take these precautions."

"Oh, yes," Peter said. "Yes indeed."

"Of course, I was delighted to put them at ease," Antonio said smiling. "I told them, quite simply, that you are my friend. That you are a distinguished, amiable, and, hopefully, a permanent resident of our village. That you are a businessman of honor and acumen; an *aficionado* of sympathy and knowledge. I mentioned you had been awarded the Order of the Blue Star by the Administration of Malaga for your work during the floods two years ago, and that you had contributed most generously to the expenses of our Virgin's trip to *their* fiesta. At the end of this, Peter, they were quite apologetic, I assure you. But still puzzled, Peter. Still puzzled."

"About what?"

The policeman smiled. "They are northerners, after all. Efficient but overly civilized. The plain explanation always eludes them. I said to their chief of security, 'Senor, I'm only a provincal policeman. But if I surprised a man seeking privacy in a deserted lane or passageway, I would not automatically assume he was a criminal. No. I would guess he had taken an extra glass of beer or so with his dinner, and had misjudged the distance from the café back to his hotel.'"

Antonio grinned and clapped Peter's shoulders.

"They hadn't thought of that! Can you imagine?"

Peter smiled too; he felt giddy with relief.

"Now they are waiting for you with open arms," the policeman said.

"They're what!"

"After the things I told them, they are eager to treat you with distinction, with special attention."

"But that's the last thing I want, Antonio."

"Don't be so modest. Call on them for anything at all, Peter. Let them provide you with an escort. Seriously, they are most anxious to look after you. As you would say in English, they want to keep an eye on you."

They shook hands. Peter got into his car. People stood up on the terrace and waved good-bye to him. Someone raised a glass.

He drove into the sun, toward the mountains, toward the sky, toward Pamplona.

9 ❧

AT FOUR O'CLOCK in the morning Peter and Francois walked quickly through the dark streets of Pamplona. It was July seventh, the day of San Fermin, and the city was like a huge bow drawn to the breaking point; trembling and eager to release its gathered energies.

Every hotel and pension in the town was packed to the walls; every table in every restaurant in the city had been booked solid for weeks.

In two hours the bombs would sound, the bulls would break for the streets, and the fiesta would explode into life; it didn't start or commence in any normal or predictable fashion, Peter remembered, at one second it *wasn't;* the next second it *was*—a sudden, roaring fact.

They turned into the Calle de La Estefeta and walked toward the plaza that spread in a semicircle about the building of the *Ayuntamiento*. Francois wore a dark suit. Peter was dressed in a heavy brown sweater and gray slacks. They both carried suitcases.

On their way to the plaza they passed laborers, a policeman, and a group of seemingly bewildered young Danes also carrying suitcases. There were nods, smiles, salutes. Peter and Francois turned off the Estefeta and were alone once again, swinging on briskly through the darkness.

When they reached the plaza, Francois put down his suitcase and studied his watch. Peter went into the narrow passageway that led to the warehouse behind the bank, and knelt before the clusters of iron grillwork covering the basement windows. It was quieter and darker in the passageway, with a chill bite in the damp air. He opened his suitcase and removed a transistor-powered chain-saw, which glittered dully in the gloom. It was ten inches long, and looked as if it had been designed for children, but its fine teeth were capable of gnawing through anything but processed steel plate.

The grillwork inclined toward the wall of the building at a forty-five degree angle. Peter sliced it from its frame in a single piece, and smeared the shiny cuts with black grease. The grillwork, angled to the wall as it was, could be replaced in its frame as neatly and firmly as a lid on a pot. Peter set it aside and drew a line on the bottom of a windowpane with a glass cutter. He covered this with transparent tape, and made three more incisions on the top and sides of the glass. When he gently prodded the pane with his fingertip, it fell open like a trap door, hinged by the strip of transparent tape. Peter put a hand through the window, found the catch and released it. He then replaced the pane of glass and secured it firmly with three more strips of tape. It would have required a close examination to reveal that the window had been tampered with. The work had taken sixty-five seconds.

Boots rang in the plaza. Someone hailed Francois. Peter froze against the wall.

"Yes, yes, I do need a room," he heard Francois say, in a much too hearty voice.

Peter crept up the passage and peered into the plaza. Francois was talking to a policeman.

"In that case, I'll take you to my brother's home," the policeman said. "It's only a cot, but you're lucky to find anything now. And it's not expensive."

"But I'm waiting for friends."

"Here? At this hour?"

"They're driving up from Madrid."

"Oh. Didn't you come into the plaza with someone else? A tall man with a suitcase?"

"A tall man?" Francois laughed pointlessly. "Yes. He's gone though. He's got a girl in town."

"Lucky fellow."

The policeman went away, his boots ringing hollowly on the cobblestones. When the sound faded to a mur-

mur, Francois wheeled and ducked into the passage alongside Peter. He was breathing hard; sweat beaded his forehead.

"Come on," Peter said, moving off into the darkness. . . .

The basement of the warehouse was immense. Peter stood behind the concealing bulk of a stone column and snapped on his flashlight. An irregularly pitched ceiling arched above them like the roof of a cave. Peter's torch formed a small pool of yellow light at his feet, and sent shadows leaping like phantoms toward the distant walls. The air was heavy and damp and motionless, like the air in a meat locker.

Peter took a compass from his pocket and turned the torch on it, and when the needle stopped flickering, he nodded to Francois, and followed the arrow through the darkness until he came to the wall that stood between him and the vaults of the bank. He checked his compass and studied the surface of the wall appraisingly. After a bit, he took out a crayon and drew on the dull-red bricks two black circles, three inches in diameter, three feet apart, and three feet above the floor.

He opened the suitcase, removed two hand-drills, gave one to Francois.

"Let's go," he said.

The drills dug and clawed with an angry sound at the stubborn bricks and mortar. Dust and powder rose and streaked their shining faces.

164

Church bells rang the quarter hours above the sleeping city, and from the streets came the voice of workers, faint and indistinct, and the thud of mallets on heavy timbers.

Francois leaned against the wall. Blood gleamed brightly from one of his knuckles.

"What is that?"

"The barricades. They're putting them up."

"Do we have enough time?"

"Yes. Keep drilling."

"How much longer, for God's sake? Look at my hands."

"Keep drilling."

Above them the city began to stir slowly and heavily, stretching itself like a great healthy animal. Water rumbled through the sewers beneath their feet, and there were muted sounds of traffic in the street. The gloom of the basement became streaked with slivers of pale light.

"Good God, do we have time?"

"Yes."

Peter knelt beside the suitcase to prepare his charges. But first he nibbled thoughtfully on a splinter of brick, attempting to learn something of its grain and porosity. He learned very little. The shot would be mainly guesswork, he knew, as he spat dust from his mouth and removed the blasting equipment from the suitcase.

Francois sucked blood from his damaged knuckles

165

and watched him with anxious eyes.

Peter placed the blasting machine behind a stone column thirty feet from the wall. He unreeled fusing wire, measured it into forty-foot lengths, and cut each section carefully and squarely with a pen-knife. Using a hand-crimper he attached their ends snugly to electric detonator caps. He measured the length and diameter of the caps with his eyes. Two inches by a quarter-inch. . . . He picked up a stick of dynamite and a dynamite punch. Holding the dynamite in his left hand, he twisted the punch into the end of it with his other, driving the wooden pin deeply into the hard brittle explosive.

Francois moved back. "You know what you're doing?"

"Yes."

When the holes were deep enough and wide enough, he screwed electric caps into them. He selected three sticks of dynamite for each charge, bound them together with friction tape, eased them carefully into the holes he and Francois had drilled into the wall. On top of the charges, he poured handfuls of loose brick and mortar, and pounded the mixture down hard with the flat of his hand.

Early light was spreading through the basement by then. Details emerged as the shadows shortened and retreated to the walls. There were empty packing cases, heaps of canvas hampers, a row of empty kegs, all of them covered with fine gray dust. There was only one door, and it was locked—as Peter had surmised it would be—from the opposite side. It looked as if nothing short of dynamite would budge it; the panels were made of heavy slabs of hardwood, with massive iron hinges covering half their surfaces.

"We have fifteen minutes," Peter said.

He knelt behind the stone column, and examined the blasting machine. Francois watched as Peter checked the plunger mechanism, the test pilot-light.

"You think it's going to work?"

"Yes. There'll be a heavy blast downward, a very little surface fragmentation. But cover your face, and stay behind the column. Now listen: We won't have time to drill for the second shot. We'll cover the dynamite with loose rock, as deep in the excavation as possible. Then we'll stow this gear away and clear out of here. Fast."

Francois studied Peter with a curious smile. The light in the basement was stronger and clearer now; it caught the flare of evil humor in his eyes, trapped that strange derisive spark that animated his commonplace features.

"And you're doing all of this for nothing," he said, in a soft, musing voice. "For nothing but some crazy notion of honor. Tell me: What is honor? What's it like?"

"It's a good feeling."

"Like the feeling after a fine dinner with excellent wines? Or like the feeling you have with a new and fas-

167

cinating woman, someone sensual and experimental, who drives you as wild as salt in a fresh wound?" Francois smiled delicately. "Is it a feeling like that?"

"No."

"Then I can't be missing very much."

"Don't knock it until you've tried it."

"You're a fool. I've found only one thing in life worth being loyal to, and that's my own flesh and blood. In this world a man can only betray himself." Francois smiled faintly. "So whatever you think, I'm no traitor. I always take good care of myself."

Peter glanced at his watch.

"I'm boring you, eh?" There was a touch of bitterness in Francois' tone. "You're the dedicated hero, and I'm the tiresome weakling. Is that what you think?"

"Why worry about it? You say loyalty and heroism are accidents. You equate honor with a good meal and a roll in the hay. That's a cozy philosophy. Cuddle up to it and make yourself comfortable."

Francois rubbed his hands together as if they had suddenly become cold. A tic pulled rhythmically at the corner of his mouth. "I wouldn't worry if everyone believed as I do. But my enemies believe in honor. Like you, they're fools."

"Francois, understand me." Peter's voice was deceptively mild, but something in his eyes sent an unpleasant chill down Francois' back. "I'm doing this job for my friends. To keep them free and alive. If I don't bring it off, they go down the drain. And so do I. But I promise you this: Before that happens, I'll break your back with my own two hands."

"Well, we want the same thing." Francois managed a shrug, a smile. "There's no need for threats. You can count on me."

The walkie-talkie Peter took from his pocket was no larger than a deck of cards. He looped it about his neck and put a hand on the plunger of the blasting machine. Then he glanced at his watch.

"We'll see," he said.

Grace held a walkie-talkie to her lips. She spoke into it sharply: "Peter? Two minutes!"

She stood at the windows of a third-floor hotel room looking down at the bull pens. In the small square facing the corral, men ranged about in excited groups, glancing from their watches to the bulls. The river curved around the scene like a silver arm, smooth and glistening in the gray morning light.

The animals milled about restlessly. Faint but clear, the brass bells of the oxen sounded on the air.

"Peter?" There was no answer; she began to pray.

"I'm reading you fine." The voice was Peter's in miniature, tiny and metallic in her ears. "How do I sound?"

"Perfect." She tightened her grip on the walkie-talkie to keep her fingers from trembling. "Did everything go all right?"

"No trouble so far."

"They're clearing the square now. The police are sending everybody out. One man is going over to the gates of the corral. He's taking the bar down."

"I've got one minute. Are we synchronized?"

"Yes. Fifty-five seconds now."

Grace pulled the curtains back and moved closer to the window. On a low platform behind the corral, a Spaniard in uniform knelt beside a plunger attached to a blasting machine. The wires trailing from it ran across the ground to the river bank, and disappeared under a metal shell which was surrounded by a fence of thick wooden posts.

"Thirty seconds," Grace said.

"What?"

"Thirty seconds." She made herself speak clearly and firmly. "Thirty seconds, darling."

"I'm ready."

"Oh, be careful."

"None of that now."

"Yes. I'll try. They're opening the gate now. The bulls are moving toward it. I love you, Peter."

"Ten seconds?"

"Yes. Peter, the bulls are starting to run! They're ready to blast."

"Five seconds?"

"Four . . . three . . . He's holding the plunger!

170

Now, Peter, *Now!*"

The old Basque town rocked with the explosion. Smoke shot out from under the huge metal shell, and rose in erratic puffs above the river.

The bulls were loose!

Grace put a hand tightly against her trembling lips and stared at the creeping second hand on her watch. In the square below the bulls charged the barricades, their neck muscles cresting with excitement and fury. The noise mounted in waves. The oxen circled the raging bulls, their huge brass bells ringing in mournful counterpoint to the joyous roars of the crowd.

The Spaniard on the platform watched the animals alertly, his hand resting on the plunger of the blasting machine.

Grace said a prayer. Then she whispered: "Peter?"

"Yes, I'm okay." He was panting so hard that Grace could barely make out the words. "It was a good shot. Three feet or more. The second's all set. What's happening?"

"The bulls are calming down. Some of them are standing with the oxen. Now the others are coming over to them. There's only one loose. A big gray and white one. He's still butting the corral gate. Peter, get ready! He's turning. He's trotting across to the other bulls."

The seven bulls formed a group flanked on all sides by lumbering oxen. A man in gray twill coveralls came out from behind the barricades and cracked a whip. He

171

turned and waved to the Spaniards on the platform.

"They're running, Peter. Running fast. Now, Peter. *Now!*"

The second blast rocked the city. The bulls were free and on their way, and the daredevils in the barricaded streets ahead of them spat in their hands for luck and took to their heels.

10 ❧

PETER HAD ANTICIPATED everything but the intensity of the noise. He had imagined the look of barricaded streets, the press of the crowd, and, with ghastly clarity, the thrusting, seeking horns of the bulls.

But he hadn't imagined a clamor like the howling of a storm, limitless and infinite. Steadily and powerfully, the roaring of the crowd grew in volume, while beneath it, like the bass of a great orchestra, the pounding hooves of the bulls shook the earth.

The sound beat on him like flails, numbing and splintering his thoughts. There was a scream in his ears.

"I can't do it."

Francois crouched against the wall of the passageway and shook his head at Peter. The words seemed to have torn his mouth; it looked like a ragged hole punched into his straining features.

173

"You've got to!"

"No, no, no."

Peter struck him across the face.

"There are no free rides," he said. Then he hit him again, using the back of his hand this time, and the impact of the blow bloodied the Frenchman's lips and drove him to his knees. Peter hauled Francois up, unlatched the barricade, opened it and booted him into the street. Francois screamed and ran. Peter leaped after him, the door of the barricade swinging shut with a crash that was lost in the crescendoing roar of the crowd.

The small plaza was like the eye of a storm, an uneasy vacuum surrounded by turbulence and noise. Every window overlooking it was packed with screaming faces. Every eye was turned to the street leading up from the river.

The *suicideros* were running now. Only a half-dozen still danced nervously about the plaza, eyes rolling back and sideways in their heads to watch for the bulls. Above the rhythmic chanting and bellowing the sound of hooves came on the air like a rumble of artillery fire.

The last of the runners were beautiful in their fear; there seemed a holiness in their terror, some sanctification of the spirit in this willing and ritualistic acceptance of dangers that no sane or prudent man would expose himself to; their smiles were straining and ghastly, but their eyes seemed brightened by the prospects of

174

grace and honor.

Everyone was shouting. The first oxen came into sight, their splayed hooves slapping and banging and slipping on the cobblestones. Then the bulls appeared and all the runners fled from the plaza.

Peter ran as he might in a nightmare. The harder he tried, the less progress he seemed to make; the air was like a physical barrier against his heaving chest, so dense and heavy that it seemed to take all his strength to force his way through it. His feet thudded ponderously, as if they were encased in lead. The street narrowed as it angled into the Estefeta, and the screams of the crowd hammered at the walls of the buildings like a cyclone trapped in a wind tunnel. From balconies and windows, thousands of white, disembodied faces floated above Peter like dangerously inflated balloons. There were thin faces, fat faces, wide faces, and long faces, all with black holes in the middle of them that seemed to be twisting and writhing in agony. Peter's ribs were like red-hot bars caging his straining lungs. He had a horrid image of an ankle giving way, a pounding heel coming down solidly on an overripe banana peel.

A young man in a white shirt and a red handkerchief about his neck shot past Peter. He looked frantically over his shoulder, his dark eyes full of wild lights. Then he screamed in transports of exquisite terror, and bolted on up the street.

175

But Peter was not alone. To his left, coming on steadily and imperturbably, were the massive horns of the lead oxen. And behind them the bulls.

A hand gripped his shoulder.

"Are you trying to be killed?"

Don Miguel, the Sword of Malaga, ran evenly alongside Peter, keeping abreast of him with the light, skipping strides of a *torero*. The people on the balconies recognized the old man and screamed at him.

"Slow down," he said to Peter.

The bulls were going past them like a freight train. There was a reek of dung and sweat, spurts of dust, and the rattle and ring of their hooves on the paving stones. Peter saw hairy nostrils and small dull eyes, lashing tails and a froth of sweat on thick pads of shoulder muscle.

"Let them go by. Slow down."

They stopped running. Peter put both hands to his heaving sides and watched the bulls pounding up the street with the oxen.

"*Amigo*, where did you come from?"

Peter gulped down air and shook his head; he couldn't speak.

"I was watching for you. I waited until the last second. Where were you standing?"

"Across the plaza, near the barricades."

"It's funny I didn't see you. Listen, if you wait until the last, try to get behind the bulls. You can't trot along

176

with them as if they were cows. It's very dangerous."

Men on the balcony began to shout at them.

Don Miguel looked away quickly. The lines in his tough old face seemed to sharpen; his eyes grew brighter. He said: "Stand very still, Peter."

A towering black and white bull was trotting back along the street. A newspaper blew under its nose. The bull chopped at it viciously. It sniffed the gutters and looked up at the shouting people in the balconies.

"Stand very quietly."

Peter didn't need the old *torero's* injunction; every joint in his body suddenly seemed to have acquired a thick, immobilizing sheath of ice. He prayed for the crowd to be silent; that was almost the worst of it, the hysterical sense-numbing noise.

The bull was twenty feet away when it noticed the two human targets standing motionless in the street. It raised its head to stare at them, and the movement caused a crest of muscle to rise steeply in its shoulders. Then it came forward in quick stops and starts, pawing delicately at the paving stones, feinting right and left with big, murderous horns, as if trying to determine whether these tall, postlike objects could be frightened or startled into action.

"Very still now," Don Miguel said, without moving his lips.

The bull stopped five feet away, and sniffed the ground. They formed a tableau under the screaming

177

crowds, the men, the animal, the noise itself, all linked together in a pattern so volatile that it seemed ready to explode at any instant of its own interior tensions. It was a foretaste of what must be the temporal texture of eternity, Peter thought with therapeutic irrelevance; seconds that were like years, minutes that were like centuries

Someone raised a first-floor window and flapped a bed sheet into the street.

The bull wheeled away from them and charged it.

Don Miguel pulled Peter along the street, then froze him with the pressure of his hand. The bull turned from the limp, unresisting, unsatisfactory sheet, and looked back at them.

"Stand very still."

Another sheet flapped temptingly from a window farther up the street.

The bull went for it at a hard gallop, ripped it free with one savage chop, and continued up the street with the big white sheet flapping and trailing beneath its churning hooves.

Don Miguel smiled at the cheering people in the balconies.

"It's like old times," he said and wiped his forehead. "Peter, you have a story to bore children with in years to come."

"What the devil are you doing here in Pamplona?"

"Let's go and drink some wine. It's not too early to

start lying about the size of those horns."

"Answer my question."

Don Miguel shrugged apologetically. "Well, there's an old Spanish proverb that goes this way: It is better to eat dry bread in the sunlight, than to join a feast in darkness."

"That isn't old, it isn't Spanish, and it isn't proverbial," Peter said.

"Very few foreigners would understand that. Come along, Peter, it's time for some wine."

"Why won't you answer my question?"

The old man scratched his ear. "All right. I came here to help you."

"You're a fool."

"You see? That's why I didn't give you an answer. A man who can't afford friends is too poor to have enemies. And a Spaniard without foes is like a bull without horns. That isn't old or Spanish or proverbial either. But think about it, anyway. Now. Will you take some wine with me?"

Peter sighed helplessly.

They went off down the street with their arms about one another's shoulders. . . .

One night later in the week, Peter met with a carpenter in a drafty shed near the river.

"I did my best, senor, but the time was short."

"I think you've done a fine job."

"Thank you. But if there were more time I would put

a sharper light in his eyes. And more of the devil in his smile. But the nose and cheeks are good. And the uniform is correct. Black, with the silver trimming on the coat and hat. It's the style of Phillip the Second, you know. Now. You see those curls on his wig? Where they come down over his left temple? Well, just behind the lowest curl is a little lever that makes the other thing work. You can hardly see it, eh, senor?"

The *Cabezuda* was propped against a wall of the shed, its fresh paint sparkling in the light of the bare bulb hanging from the ceiling. Under comically arched brows, its great black eyes were fixed fiercely at a point about six feet above Peter's head. The pink cheeks were bigger than pumpkins. A splayed nose hung suspended over ruby-red lips which were stretched wide in a gleefully ferocious smile. The tricorn hat, austerely formal in its trimmings of black and silver, was pulled down raffishly over one eye. A drum hung from a strap around the neck, the sticks secured to the rim by loops of tasseled green cord. From the shoulders, folds of dark cloth dropped to the ground. The hems were bound with red flannel, on which sequins glittered in cabalistic patterns.

"Look!" The carpenter raised the folds of cloth and showed Peter the single four-by-four which supported the frame of the *Cabezuda*. Attached to this post, at right angles to the ground, was a yoke padded with leather.

180

"Watch!" The carpenter crouched and fitted his head through the yoke. When he stood erect the *Cabezuda* rose another two feet in the air.

Peter stared appraisingly at its eyes. They were now at least eight feet above his own.

"It's fine," he said. "Perfect."

He gave the happy artisan a bonus for his industry, and sent him off smiling.

From every quarter of the town came the sounds of the fiesta. Music and singing and the noise of firecrackers, faint and joyous on the air. But it was the joy of other hearts, and it did nothing to gladden Peter's. The shed was a comfortable haven, it seemed to him, against a mindless sort of gaiety he wasn't able to join in.

He sat and smoked a cigarette. It was good to rest and think of nothing. He was not tired, but he was curiously discouraged.

The night before he had quarreled with Grace. She had been dressed for dinner in a gown the color of ivory, a saucy little diamond tiara crowning her smooth blonde head.

"It's charming," he had said. "Where did you ever pick up a thing like that?"

"Oh? It didn't occur to you that I might have bought it?"

"Grace, you know what I mean."

"I most certainly do."

That had been the start of it. He had tried to make amends, to conciliate her, by explaining in generous terms that he didn't give a damn about her soul any more. That he couldn't care less about it. This had caused her indignation to balloon into anger. Then she had begun to weep, which had infuriated him, and from that point on their evening had deteriorated swiftly and disastrously.

There was a tap on the door of the shed.

He rose and let Angela and Phillip in.

"Is it all right?" she asked, glancing at the *Cabezuda*.

"I won't know till we try it."

Her small face was pale and irritable. "Let's get on with it then."

"Is something wrong?"

"I feel quite ill, thank you. A goat wouldn't touch the slops you're making me eat. The milk tastes like gruel that's gone bad. The crackers choke me."

"Okay, Phillip," Peter said, without quite smiling.

"Yes," Phillip said, in the tone he would have used in replying to a question.

Angela looked at him sharply, but obviously read nothing in his broad impassive face. She shrugged and swung herself onto his shoulders. She wore black leotards, a tight black jersey sweater, and patent leather slippers, a costume which so completely stripped her of sex that she looked like a slim and agile boy attempting a balancing trick with an indulgent adult.

182

Phillip carried her to the *Cabezuda*.

"All right, Angela," Peter said. "Behind the lowest curl of the wig there's a lever. Push it to the right as far as you can."

"This knob?"

"Yes."

Angela pushed the knob hard, and one side of the *Cabezuda* slid open, like the door of a cupboard.

"Get in," Peter said.

Phillip hoisted her into the air. She crawled into the *Cabezuda*, squeezed herself into a ball, and pushed the side of the *Cabezuda* back into place.

"Angela, can you hear me?"

"Yes." Her voice was muffled but clear.

"There's another opening in back. See if it works."

Angela's face appeared high above them in an aperture in the rear of the *Cabezuda*. The second opening was only six inches square.

"Okay, Phillip," Peter said.

Phillip stooped and fitted his head and neck into the yoke under the *Cabezuda*. The folds of cloth fell about his legs to the ground, concealing all of him but the tips of his boots.

He stood erect and lost his balance. The *Cabezuda* swayed sideways. From inside it came a sound like the hissing of a terrified cat.

Peter braced the head with his hands.

"All right, Phillip, try again."

They practiced for an hour. It was an hour in which the big Frenchman attempted stops, starts, and turns; walked backwards and sideways; and managed at last to trot heavily about the little shed, as rhythmically as a draft horse in a circus. It was an hour in which Peter's spirits rose slightly.

When they were ready to leave, Angela touched his hand, unexpectedly, and said, "May I talk to you a minute?"

"Phillip, I'll call you tomorrow."

"Yes. Goodnight."

"What is it, Angela?"

"I'm sorry I was rude. It's just nerves. Would you like to come over to the hotel? I'll buy you a drink."

"I have several things to attend to."

"Well, can we sit down then? I'm exhausted."

There was a wooden bench against the wall. Angela stretched her legs and arched her back gratefully. The tight black jersey yielded to the thrust of her small, hard breasts. "Oh, that's a good feeling. It's strange inside that thing. You lose all sense of direction. I mean, you don't know whether you're going forward or backward or sideways. Added to that is a strange feeling I have about Phillip. I think, Peter, that he'd enjoy throwing that big head into the river with me inside it." She relaxed and put her feet up on a packing case. The white skin of her fragile ankles gleamed between black slacks and slippers; the illusion was a curious one, for in the strong but uncertain light, it seemed as if she were delicately fettered by her own flesh. "Do you have a cigarette?"

Peter gave her a cigarette and lighted it.

"Peter, do you think it's going to work?"

"I think there's a good chance."

She smiled at him. "This is like old times, isn't it?"

"In a way, I suppose it is."

"But you know, I'm worried about Francois."

"Why?"

"Well—" She hesitated and shrugged lightly. "He doesn't trust you, Peter."

"We have only two more shots to make," he said quietly. "On Sunday morning we reach the vault. If he doesn't have the film with him, I won't blow it. So he had better trust me; he doesn't have any choice."

"I know, I know," she said irritably. "I'd give you the films tonight, this minute, if it were up to me. But he wouldn't hear of it." She turned and stared into his eyes, and for an instant there was such a rosy innocence in her face, such a childish and wistful look about her slightly parted lips, that Peter felt a reluctant twinge of nostalgia for those long-ago days when he had believed there might be something precious, something salvagable, beyond the delicate and exquisite camouflage of her beauty.

"Tell me one thing, Peter," she said. "Just one thing. Do you think I'm a rotten bitch for getting you into

185

this? Or can you understand that I had to?"

"Let's not go into that, okay?"

"Do you still feel anything at all for me?" She blew delicately on the tip of her cigarette, a gentle smile radiating from her lips to her eyes. The cigarette flared rosily, and she said, "Anything like that, Peter? Any little spark a chance wind could make warm and beautiful again?"

"Let's don't go into that either," he said drily.

"I see. It's all for Grace now. Do you love her so much that you can't spare even a kind thought for me?"

Peter listened to the sounds of the fiesta drifting on the night winds over the river. A rocket went off with a crash. There was a machine-gun rattle of fireworks. Angela was smiling at him, the soft curve of her lips benign and voluptuous.

"All right, cut out the act," he said. "What do you want?"

"I don't know what you mean."

"Stop waving your breasts at me. Stop the auld lang syne bit. What's wrong?"

She sighed. "If I didn't have that film, I'd be frightened of you. I wish I knew how you did it. It's Francois. He's losing his nerve."

"He was all right this morning. What happened?"

"I'm not quite sure. It was at lunch. A car drove by on the other side of the square from the café we were sitting at. It was a gray Citroen. When Francois saw it,

186

he spilled his wine down his shirt. He told me the driver looked like someone he had trouble with in Algeria. I don't know about what. It was cards or women, I suppose. But he's been drinking ever since. I told you he didn't trust you. Now he doesn't trust me either."

"So you thought we might join forces, and kick him out into the cold. Is that it?"

"I'd sleep with the devil for those diamonds," she said quietly. "Do I have to tell you that?" She looked at him with hard, bitter eyes. "You don't want me, that's obvious. Francois won't for much longer. Can you imagine how it will be when I'm older? Without money? Saying *please* to drunken students? Saying *please* to old men who beg you to be naughty so they can beat you?" Her voice was suddenly ragged; an ugly fear glittered deep in her eyes. "Saying *please* to the whole rotten world? Crying to it for mercy?"

"Where is Francois?"

"In the Castillo, drinking. He wouldn't stay alone at the hotel."

"Let's go."

She smiled ironically. "I see how touched you are by my problems."

"You're worrying about the future. That's a luxury I can't afford."

"You may wish you had, dear."

Peter filed the remark away in a compartment of his mind, which he thought of as a repository for ticking

187

bombs. Then he turned off the lights in the shed and they walked up the bank of the river toward the Plaza del Castillo.

Francois said: "So what have you two been cooking up?" He was drinking brandy. "Or were you strolling about the town like sweethearts?" He smiled coldly at Angela. "Did he tell you your body was made by glass-blowers and magicians?"

"Shut up," she said.

"I will not shut up!"

They had found him at a table on the terrace of the Café Kutz, seated with his back to a wall, a half-dozen saucers stacked before him. Peter glanced at the drink Francois was holding.

"I'd advise you to make that a nightcap."

"When I want your advice, I'll ask for it."

The plaza was boiling with noise and excitement. Fireworks erupted from the small park in the middle of the square. Red and white Roman candles raced toward the sky with huge *whooshing* explosions, and disintegrated into a billion gaudy patterns high in the darkness. The streets and sidewalks were thick with reeling tourists and Spaniards, all slung with goatskins of wine. Weaving snakelines of dancers clogged traffic. Dozens of *Cabezudas* swayed high above the heads of the crowd. Some were made up as devils and witches, others as clowns and bishops and gypsies. Fire-bulls, *toros* built of papier-mâché, belched flame from their nostrils, shot sparkling puffballs of smoke from their hollow horns. The incessant pound of explosives mingled with the brassy thud of marching bands.

This was the sound of San Fermin, rhythmic, huge, incessant. It was as if rubber truncheons were beating against the underside of the earth; the sounds seemed to explode underneath the feet, and go rocking and blasting up the legs and spine, to burst inside the head.

The terraces of all the cafés ringing the plaza were jammed with tourists. Tables were thick with bottles and glasses and saucers. Everyone was calling for drinks. The waiters squeezed themselves torturously through the crowds, flushed and sweating, trays balanced precariously over their heads.

Snippets of talk rustled about Peter's ears like scraps of paper in a gale.

"—*if you drink that I'm going back to the hotel.*"

"—*Hemingway said Cagnacho was yellow. Look it up, Old buddy, look it up.*"

"—*it's a goddamn shame the way they spoil these places.*"

"—*didn't come here to sit in a hotel and watch you write postcards.*"

"—*I didn't say he was yellow, Hemingway did.*"

"—*Left Bank, the Dome and Select, even the Village, they've spoiled all of it.*"

"—*lot he knew.*"

"—*sure, Chicago used to be a good town.*"

"—*you shouldn't have done that, dear. Waiter? You really shouldn't. Just remember to tell Dr. Abrams about this little indulgence. Don't conveniently forget it, dear. Waiter!*"

"—*then why did he shoot himself, buster?*"

Francois ordered another brandy. He wore sunglasses and a cap pulled down low on his forehead, but Peter sensed that his eyes were flicking intently and nervously about the terrace of the café.

"I have been very trusting, very cooperative," Francois said in a thick, angry voice. "Good Francois. He lies in the sun, not a worry in his head. Tell him this, tell him that, he nods and smiles and does what he's told. But I'm not a fool."

"Who said you were?"

"How do we leave the bank Sunday morning?"

"I told you twice. The old storm drains run under the bank. They're dry this time of year. We will follow them to the river."

"Then why do we give the things to her?"

"Because there's an elbow of the drain that's only fourteen inches wide."

"I'm tired of your clever plans. I'm sick of hearing how smart and formidable you are. You're doing this for nothing but honor? And Phillip? He takes a little money, but very little. And he's not the least curious about what we're after. And your woman, that great iceberg, she is working for nothing too. Just like that crazy old bullfighter. I'm smothered by this philanthropy. I ask myself why you're so good to me, so charitable."

"Francois, this is no time for trouble," Angela said quietly.

"No, good faithful Francois mustn't make trouble! I must do what I'm told, like a well-trained dog. I'm sick of it. I'm sick of being ordered about by this clever, dangerous thief, the famous Black Dove."

Peter gripped the neck of the brandy bottle. "Listen, Francois," he said very quietly. "If you don't shut up now, I'm going to knock all your front teeth down your throat."

"But—"

"I said shut up."

A roar like a mighty wave washed over the plaza. From the balconies, floodlights swept across the crowds in the streets, cutting so swiftly and blindingly through the darkness, and in such intricate and dazzling patterns, that the effect was as fantastic and impressive as great swords swinging in the hands of giants.

Everyone was standing, climbing onto chairs and tables.

To a roaring drumbeat, the Virgins of Spain were entering the Plaza del Castillo, borne on massive and dazzlingly decorated floats by hundreds of proud attendants.

Angela stood on tiptoe, straining to see, and the glitter in her eyes was no less vivid than the blaze of the jewels on the arms and throats of the Virgins.

Each float was surrounded by a cordon of police and soldiers. When the platforms dipped and swayed with the rhythmically lurching strides of the men supporting them, the motion caused sparkling eruptions from the gems and jewels hung about the statutes of the Virgins.

Everyone was cheering. In stately sequence, and to mounting applause, the serenely expressionless statues were carried about the square, bathed in brilliance from the spotlights. The Blue Tears of Santa Eulalia, gleaming at the throat of the Virgin of Granada, earned an ovation. They were followed by the Golden Oars of Navarre, the Silver Slippers of Saint Peter, and the Tears of Christ—incredible rubies supported on golden pilasters. Then a gasp of admiration swept the plaza like a sudden gale, as the Diamond Flutes of Carlos and the Countess of Altamira's Net and Trident of diamonds were borne into the square.

Peter studied them thoughtfully. Angela's eyes were on fire.

The Flutes of Carlos were not musical instruments, but exquisite silver columns whose miniature Doric capitals were studded with square-cut diamonds. There were three of these, each eleven inches long, and each worth, Peter estimated, about a million dollars on the fence market, and perhaps three times that if it were possible to sell them honorably over the counters of Cartier's or Tiffany's.

The pliable gold mesh which secured the Net of diamonds was hung like a wedding veil on the smooth plaster brow of the Virgin of Seville. In her arms was the Trident of diamonds. The Trident symbolized the Holy Trinity of the Catholic faith, and each of its tines was capped by a diamond, of a size and perfection, chosen, it was understood, to represent the relative status of the personages of the Divine Triumvirate. The Father's was the largest; the Son's was next in size, while the Holy Ghost's was the smallest of the three, but any one of them, Peter thought, was big enough to use as a doorstop.

Theologians had explained these disparities in size variously; some held that the Divine Spirit, being pure essence, was best served and symbolized by the smallest stone; others insisted that the difference was seeming, not real, since all material riches were the same, i.e., nothing, in the eyes of the Lord; a modern view had it that the overshadowing of the Son by the Father was apostate and Oedipal; but another camp (the syndicalists) argued that the Son and Spirit (Worker, Union) were conclusively greater than the Father (the State), and while this was interesting in theory, its application in the area of practical politics had landed quite a few people in jail.

A waiter touched Peter's arm. "A note for you, senor."

Peter read it and frowned. Francois was watching him.

"Who gave you this?" Peter asked the waiter.

"A man. Over there." He waved with a suggestion of total frustration and impotence toward masses of people on the opposite side of the terrace. "Over there. A man."

Peter saw no one he recognized. He put the note in his pocket.

"Excuse me," he said to Angela. To Francois, he said, "Same time tomorrow morning. Don't be late."

Then he hurried off. But as he fought his way through the crowds in the plaza, someone hailed him by name.

"Peter. I knew I'd come across you. What wonderful luck!"

Antonio Gonzalez y Najera, the policeman of their village, smiled broadly and pounded Peter's shoulders with rough affection.

"I asked for you at the Administration of Police. I thought you would call on them."

"I've been busy, Antonio. What the devil are you doing in Pamplona?"

"I am guarding, if you will forgive my using an important word for an unnecessary task, I am guarding our Virgin's trinkets. Here she comes now. Bringing up the rear, with hardly a thousand pesetas worth of finery on her poor head."

The small float which supported the Virgin of Santa Maria was brilliant with flowers. There were wild poppies, marguerite daisies, tiny blue iris, mimosa, carnations, and roses. Sprays of jasmine, the tiny trumpet blossoms waxen and fragrant, formed a double border around the float.

In the arms of the Virgin was a bouquet of white roses. In her simplicity and dignity, it seemed to Peter that she represented something of Spain that was not quite reflected in the opulence of her grand sisters.

The applause for her was warm and affectionate.

"She's getting quite a hand, Antonio."

"I beg your pardon?"

"Listen to the applause."

The policeman dismissed it with a shrug. "It's a sentimental response. Patronizing and contented. It's like the millionaire on the terrace of his villa smiling wistfully at the fishermen toiling below him on the beach. Ah, how he envies them! Such purity and innocence! But in his heart he is very glad not to be burdened with such innocence. Let's have some wine, Peter."

"I've got to meet someone. How about tomorrow?"

"I'll look for you."

195

The hotel, the Aguilar, was in the new quarter of the city. Peter rode to the third floor in an elevator, hurried along a clean, carpeted corridor, rapped on a door. It was opened by Morgan.

"Oh, Peter, I knew you'd come. I knew you wouldn't desert me."

"What kind of trouble have you got yourself into?"

"The very worst kind, Peter." Morgan's sigh caused his stomach to swell out like a sail in a great wind. "The very worst!"

"Your note said someone was trying to kill you. Is that on the level?"

He walked into the room. Morgan stepped aside and closed the door. Something hard prodded Peter's spine.

From behind him, Blake said: "Take it nice and easy now. If you think this is a gun, go to the head of the class."

Tonelli appeared in the doorway of the adjoining bedroom.

"Hello, Mr. Churchman," he said with a faint smile. He held a forty-five automatic in his right hand with a suggestion of familiarity and competence. "As my pal suggested, take it nice and easy. You're going to be our guest for a couple of days."

11 ∽

In GRACE'S ROOM, Francois looked bitterly at Angela. "It's not puzzling to me, not in the least. He's run out on us. I think that should be clear enough by now."

"You may be right. But it isn't like him."

"You're both talking like fools," Grace said. "You know Peter wouldn't quit. Something's happened to him."

"Yes, of course," Francois said, in a voice suddenly high and rigid with emotion. "And I'll tell you what it was. He knew I was onto him."

Grace looked helplessly at the walkie-talkie she still held in her hand. It was a mute link to Peter, an earnest token of her faith in him, and she hadn't been able to put it aside. But hours had gone by and there was no word from him. Not a whisper.

"Oh, damn him," Angela said, more in weariness than

anger. "Even if he came back, it wouldn't matter. We missed our chance today."

Francois had been looking intently at Grace.

"Now listen: He received a note in the Castillo last night. It disturbed him. Or he meant me to think it disturbed him. I don't know which. What do you know about it?"

"Why, nothing at all," Grace said.

"You're quite sure?"

"Of course."

Francois smiled faintly. "You're getting nothing from this? And neither is Peter? The risk, the danger, are all debts owed to honor, eh? Well, I doubt it very much."

"What do you think?" Angela asked him.

"Perhaps they want the diamonds for themselves."

"Oh, you're an idiot," Grace said. "We're wasting time. We've got to go out and look for him. He may be lying unconscious in a hospital, or in jail."

"Yes," Francois said drily. "And while we run about the town searching for him, what will he be up to?" He smiled. "No, I don't like that idea. So unless you tell me the truth, I am going to do something very unpleasant to you." Still smiling, he explained the details of techniques he had seen employed on stubborn natives in Algeria, and when he had finished, Grace, who was rather pale by then, said, "Well, I shouldn't like that at all. It sounds most disagreeable."

"Then be intelligent. Cooperate with us."

"Very well. I'm an awful coward about things like that. Peter said if anything unexpected happened I was to give you two things." Grace picked up a copy of the magazine *Espana* from a coffee table and gave it to Angela. "This was one of them."

"Did he tell you what I was to look for?"

"He said that you would know."

"And the second thing?"

"It's here on the dresser." Grace's slim, dark skirt whispered lightly as she hurried across the room. Sunlight the color of ripe lemons gleamed brightly on the white bow at her throat and lent a pale liquid sheen to her nylons. She fumbled with combs and brushes, and then pulled open a drawer with a suggestion of haste and desperation. But when she found what she wanted, and spun around to face them, her eyes were cold, and something small and deadly glittered in her hand. It was a twenty-five caliber automatic, decorated with mother-of-pearl handgrips.

She said quietly: "This throws high and to the right. Francois, if you take another step toward me, I'll aim for the middle of your left thigh. I'm a good enough shot to put a very painful cloud over your technical qualifications to manhood."

Francois seemed to be trying to smile, but he only succeeded in flattening his lips, for the steady blue shine of the muzzle was not less unnerving than the light in Grace's eyes.

Angela threw the magazine on the floor and stamped on it.

Grace picked up the telephone. When the operator answered, she gave her a number in rapid Spanish. . . .

Peter watched the first fragile lights of dawn rising on the horizon. It was Sunday morning, and in a few more hours the bulls would be running for the last time in this fiesta of San Fermín.

It was all over now. . . .

He and Morgan shared a sofa. Tonelli sat facing them with a gun in his hand. He looked alert and wary, despite the long vigil, but he also wore a "sportsman's" ring, and cords knotted with a jeweled clasp in lieu of a tie, and Peter could not believe he was a serious man. Blake stood at a table against the wall making himself a drink. He was the hairy one, with the bunched-up features, the head pointed like an artillery projectile, the fingers like bananas.

"Peter, I'm dreadfully sorry," Morgan said, for perhaps the fiftieth time.

"Knock it off, Fatso," Blake said.

"I was merely trying to explain that if Quince hadn't taken such a conservative view of things, we might—"

"Okay, okay," Tonelli said, cutting him off irritably.

It was still dark outside and through the darkness came occasional flashes of fireworks like heat lightning, and on the air drifted the muffled sounds of marching bands and pounding drums. But the fiesta of San Fermin was drawing to a close; tomorrow's bullfight would end it. And already the hikers were buying bread and sausage and wine for their rucksacks, and charting courses north and south through gorges with rushing green streams that would take them on to Biarritz or Madrid. Tomorrow the roads fanning out from Pamplona would be clogged with cars and motorcycles, and in the strange silence that would settle in their wake, the Basques would reclaim their old town, reclaim their tables in the cafés, and by nightfall the debris of the fiesta would be sluiced away by watering trucks, and nothing would be left of these explosions of emotion and hilarity but clean, damp streets shining under the old stars.

It was all over for San Fermin and Pamplona, all over for Peter Churchman. The most audacious undertaking of his career, and perhaps the most honorable, had been smashed by these improbably authentic hoodlums, who had forced him to call Mr. Shahari and ask him to bring twenty-five thousand dollars to Pamplona. Shahari had been dubious at first, but friendship had prevailed at last; he had agreed to take the risk, to accept the possibility of being put out of business and into prison by the Spanish government, which allowed him to deal in money in the south for the sake of the tourists, but which sternly forbade him to set a foot farther north than the town of Granada.

Tonelli glanced at his watch. "You're sure you can trust this guy, Shahari?"

"He's a reliable person," Peter said.

"You'd better pray he shows," Blake said.

"May I wash my hands?" Peter asked a bit later.

"You just did," Blake said irritably.

"It's nerves, I expect."

"Come on."

Peter walked to the bathroom with Blake's gun at his back. He turned on both taps in the hand-basin, and, with but little hope, took the walkie-talkie from his pocket and tried to raise Grace. They hadn't found the set when they searched him; it had been concealed and padded by a handkerchief in the rear pocket of his trousers. But it might have been at the bottom of the sea for all the good it had done him.

But even so, there was a lonely consolation in her silence. For it was Peter's fervent hope that she had prudently packed up and cleared out of town. He whispered her name twice but the speaker remained silent. With a sigh, he put the walkie-talkie away and returned to the living room.

"Peter, they said you were a lawyer, and I had an uneasy feeling about lawyers at the time."

"That's all right. It doesn't matter."

The phone rang and Blake picked up the receiver. After listening for a second, his expression sharpened and he glanced at Tonelli. "It's the desk clerk. He says what's-his-name's in the lobby. Shahari. But he wants to talk to Churchman."

"Okay," Tonelli said to Peter. "Tell him to come up. Don't put any English on it. Just get him up here."

Peter rose and took the phone from Blake, who moved behind him and put a gun against his spine.

Peter said, "Mr. Shahari?"

"Yes, Peter." It was a low and pleasant voice, pitched just above a whisper. Peter felt his heart lurch abruptly. If he were a camel, he thought, with a dizzying irrelevance, he would now be lying flat with a broken back; for this was the last straw.

"Well, hello," he said.

"Darling, can you talk?" Grace said softly.

"As a matter of fact, I can't."

Blake's gun dug into his back. "Cut the chatter."

"Excuse me a second." Peter covered the phone and looked evenly at Tonelli and Blake. "If you don't want to blow this deal sky-high, you'd better listen. He's got the wind up. He wants me to meet him in the lobby. Alone. You heard me tell him I can't. I'd better explain I'm not dressed. Anything. But let me talk to him. Perhaps I can calm him down."

They exchanged dubious glances, but before they reached a decision, Peter spoke again into the phone. "As a matter of fact, Mr. Shahari, I just stepped out of the shower. Why don't you come on up?"

"Do you mean that?"

"Oh, no," Peter said smiling.

"I understand," Grace whispered rapidly. "I called Mr. Shahari yesterday. I thought you might have needed tools or equipment. It was all I could think of. He told me what you'd asked him to do, where he was meeting you. How many are there?"

"Oh, two, I should say."

"Keep on talking."

"Well, I'm sorry I put you to so much trouble." Peter winked at Tonelli and Blake, who were watching him with uncertain frowns. "Excuse me a second." He covered the phone. "This is better. He's explaining the difficulties he had raising the money."

"Then get him up here," Tonelli said sharply.

"I'm trying my best. But he doesn't like doing business this way. He prefers a café or restaurant." Peter spoke to Grace. "Well, all's well that ends well. You have the money?"

"Peter, Mr. Shahari's not coming. I told him not to. Was that all right?"

"Why, that's fine."

"Don't be angry, but I did something else."

"Really?"

"Yes. I—I called Mr. Bendell and the Irishman. They're here."

"Now that was enterprising of you. I wouldn't have thought of it. Or even considered it, as you must realize."

"Please, darling. I had no choice. I knew what was at

204

stake. And they wanted to help. They blasted yesterday morning. We can reach the vault on schedule."

"Well, Godamnit," Peter said weakly.

Blake's gun dug into his spine. "No more chatter. If he doesn't want to come up, I'm going down and get him."

"Good," Peter said into the phone. "I'll expect you right away."

He dropped the receiver into its cradle, and rubbed his hands together briskly. Now a humble submission to the designs of fate seemed in order.

"Listen carefully," he said to Tonelli and Blake. "I'll explain to Mr. Shahari that you are business associates of mine. So put those guns out of sight and button your jackets. I want you to look as proper as possible."

Seemingly mesmerized by his crisp injunctions, Tonelli and Blake stuffed their guns into their belts and buttoned their jackets over them.

"But how about Fatso?"

"That's all right. Mr. Shahari knows Morgan."

Peter hesitated an instant, frowning indecisively. Then he thought, to hell with the Irishman, let him find his own fun, and with that decision firmly and unalterably in mind, Peter kicked Tonelli in the stomach, and struck Blake across the jugular with a cutting chop of his hand.

There was a discreet tap on the door.

Peter took no chances with Blake. He pumped three rights into his stomach, and these made it imperative for Blake to breathe, but the damage to his throat made it difficult for him to do so; the combination of conflicting interests caused him to sink to the floor, trying earnestly to stay alive until he could get some air into his lungs. Tonelli was well out of it.

Peter took their guns from them and went to the door.

With some difficulty, Morgan managed to get Grace aside, away from Peter, and when he had her attention he pointed to the Irishman, and said shrewdly: "He's not Mr. Shahari. Neither is the little fat one. Shouldn't we tell Peter?"

"I believe he knows," Grace said with a gentle smile. "But there's something else you might do for him."

"Oh, I'd do anything for Peter."

Peter was looking at his watch. "All right, chums, let's get with it."

The Irishman stopped in the doorway and looked back enviously at Blake and Tonelli. "Peter, you're a selfish bastard. Wouldn't you even wait one minute for an old pal?"

"Come on," Peter said sharply.

For the church bells were already sounding five, and a dangerous dawn was spreading slowly down from the hills to cover the old town with a light the color of pearls.

But it was not yet too late. . . .

12 ❧

GRACE'S VOICE sounded suddenly in his ear, a tense, metallic whisper.

"Get ready, Peter. They're opening the gate. The bulls are running."

Peter gripped the handle of the plunger, and looked at Bendell and the Irishman. "Here we go, lads."

"Now, Peter! *Now.*"

Peter rammed the plunger home, and two explosions shook the air, their echoes blending and converging instantly in one great blast; the first roared over their heads like long freight trains rumbling toward the sky, while the second, compact and contained, sounded deep within the shaft they were driving through the wall to the bank. A jet of smoke and dust shot into the basement. Splinters of rock whistled and whined about their ears.

The Irishman and Bendell, carrying short pickaxes, ran through the eddying layers of smoke, and disappeared into the mouth of the tunnel. Francois and Peter followed with a toolkit and valises. Another explosion sounded above the city, as the bulls began their last race through the barricaded streets. In the narrow shaft, they could hear the muffled sound of their hooves, the distant roaring of the crowds.

The Irishman's pick rang against crumbling brick and stone.

"Pay dirt, lad," he called back to Peter.

They pulled aside the last bricks with their hands chopped through lathings and plaster, and crawled, one by one, into the dark basement of the bank. Peter stood perfectly still, a hand on the Irishman's shoulders, and cut the blackness around him with the beam of his flashlight. They were in the records storage area, a vast, low-ceilinged chamber which ran parallel to the ancient boiler room and cellars on the ground floor of the bank. Wooden file cabinets stood in rows higher than their heads, and the walls were shelved and lined with musty ledgers and lock-boxes bound with metal strips.

Peter could taste the dryness on the air; it was as if the very act of their breathing had stirred dust motes lying undisturbed for decades.

The silence was complete. Peter examined it in layers, letting his ears test first the quiet of the storage area, then the adjoining cellars and boiler rooms, and finally the vault floor above their heads.

The only sound he heard was Francois' erratic breathing.

Peter squeezed the Irishman's shoulders, and moved off swiftly toward the front of the bank, following the bright, narrow path traced by his flashlight. The door sealing the storage area was tall and massive, patterned with squares of deeply carved wood. It was very old, and so was its lock, and Bendell solved the problems of its tumblers in seconds with a thin screwdriver wrapped in a handkerchief. Peter let the door swing slowly open of its own weight, and peered through a crack into the foyer of the bank.

The foyer extended the full width of the building, abutting directly onto the street, its tall arched windows and doors laced with grillwork and covered now with drawn green shades. The side walls of smooth, veined marble were flanked by tubs of dark green plants, strange and exotic in the gloomy darkness, and they gave off an earthy, verdant odor that was jarringly alive after the dry, dead air of the records room.

From the middle of the foyer a broad marble staircase rose to the second floor of the bank, eighteen worn steps with brass handrails on either side of them.

On the sidewalk, in front of the massive double doors, stood a detail of police; Peter could see their figures silhouetted against the long green shades.

Peter opened the door enough to slip through it.

With an eye on the double doors at the entrance of the bank, he ran at a half-crouch to the foot of the stairs. He sat on the first step, a valise and tool kit in his lap, squeezed himself close to the handrailing, and went up the stairs backward, easing himself from one step to the next, like a child who hadn't learned to walk, but keeping his eyes fixed all the while on the silhouetted figures of the police in the street. Francois came after him, and then Bendell and the Irishman, and there was no sound at all but the rough whisper of heavy trousers on cold marble.

On the second floor, safe from view, Peter stopped again to test the silence. Nothing moved, nothing stirred, except dust motes dancing in the dim light. There were faint traffic noises, and the distant noise of the fiesta from the street, but the air around them was as still and quiet as that in a tomb.

The second floor of the bank was vast and dim. The murky sunlight that filtered through the green shades on the windows coated everything with a translucent gloss; the rows of empty desks and ancient typewriters, the shining marble flooring and the great steel door of the vault, all shimmered with pale marine illuminations.

In the heavy, oppressive silence, an old-fashioned wall clock ticked solemnly and sturdily, its pendulum swinging with a sense of inevitability behind a glass door brightened with golden lettering advertising an insurance company. Peter flicked a glance at his Patek-Phillipe. The wall clock was slow, by almost forty-five seconds.

"Let's hit it," he said.

They hurried to the vault and commenced work with an apparently effortless precision and economy. Peter flipped open the two valises, while Bendell spread a long and narrow strip of chamois-cloth, arranging drills and bits and braces in the order they might need them, his hands moving as deftly and precisely as those of a surgeon at an operating table. The diamond teeth that ringed the cutter bar gleamed in the dim light. Peter ran his fingertips over them appraisingly, and studied the massive door of the vault.

"It's a tricky brute," he said quietly to the Irishman. "If you smash the main tumbler links, they trip the auxiliaries."

The Irishman nodded. "True, lad. And if you smash those auxiliary bastards, they set off the emergency system."

"You must work backward," Bendell said. "First the emergencies. Then the auxiliaries. The main tumbler links last."

"Don't teach your grandfather how to suck eggs," the Irishman said, with a hard grin. He rubbed his hands together for a few seconds, and picked up a punch and drill. "How much time left, Peter?"

"One hour and forty-five minutes."

"It won't be a milk run, lad. Let's get cracking."

"Hold it one second." Peter turned to Francois. "Let's have it. This is as far as we go without it."

"But of course." Francois opened his jacket, removed the can of film from under his arm, and gave it to Peter with an ironical little smile. "I'm satisfied with our bargain. Why shouldn't I be?"

Peter inspected the impress of his ring in the candle wax that smoothly sealed the locks and catches on the can of film.

"Okay, Paddy, hit it," he said, and put the film in his tool kit.

The Irishman began drilling. Peter went quickly through the gloomy light to the front windows of the bank. He moved a shade a half-inch with his fingertip, and peered out into an empty street shining with thin sunlight. This was the business district of the old town, and its buildings were sturdy and respectable, with barred windows and brass name-plates studded to the walls beside their doorways.

Twelve feet below Peter—on the sidewalk in front of the bank—was a detail of six policemen. Since the beginning of the fiesta, there was no minute of the day or night when the doors of the bank were left unguarded; a round-the-clock security was maintained by severe, alert officers with holstered automatics in their belts, and whistles hanging on short chains from the epaulets of their tunics.

This was an area of the operation Peter had never been satisfied with, although he knew from observation that at this time of morning the sunlight on the panes of glass silvered them like mirrors. In addition, the heavy squares of iron grillwork on the windows would provide a shield for what he must do now; but he was still gambling recklessly on the strength of all the slender threads of chance. The fly buzzing about a policeman's ear, or the sudden crick in the neck, that could cause a man to turn suddenly and look directly up at the window Peter was working on.

Peter drew a deep breath, and held half of it, steadying himself as he would if he were about to squeeze off a shot on a target range. Then he opened the tool kit and picked up his glass cutter. He moved the shade, slipped his hand behind it, and made a swift, precise incision on the bottom of a pane of glass. After waiting a full minute, he covered the cut with transparent tape. One of the policemen looked along the street, his eyes roving about alertly. Peter let the shade swing gently back into place, an instant before the policeman turned and glanced up at the windows of the bank. This Peter didn't like; there was literally no defense against intuition. He knew the man hadn't heard or seen anything to rouse his suspicions. But nevertheless, his hackles were up.

Peter waited several minutes before peering out again, and then he cursed softly, for he had almost missed an opportunity to finish the job in complete safety. An old man, who was obviously drunk, had fallen in the gutter, and several of the policemen were assisting him to his feet, while the others watched their efforts with indulgent smiles. But even so, Peter was able to make two more incisions, along the sides of the pane, before the policemen returned to their posts in front of the bank. He was forced to wait fifteen more minutes before making the last cut at the top of the glass. In the middle of the pane he pasted an inch-long strip of tape, with one half of it sticking up in the air. This would serve as a door handle; when he pulled on it the pane would fall backward into his hand, hinged by the transparent tape along the bottom edge of the glass.

Peter closed his tool kit and stood perfectly still for a moment. Then he looked at his hands. They had not quite stopped trembling.

The Irishman drilled four holes around the combination knob, lining them up at the cardinal compass points. Into these he inserted spring clamps which locked the diamond cutter-bar tightly against the surface of the vault door. Bendell screwed a short steel handle into the outer ring of the cutting rig.

"What's the time, Peter?" the Irishman said sharply. He had removed his jacket, and the back of his shirt was dark with perspiration. A tangle of thick black hair fell over his forehead.

"Forty-eight minutes," Peter said. He was studying the notes he had copied from documents in the Museum of Archives, analyzing certain measurements in relationship to the swinging needle of the compass he held in his hand.

"The emergency system's had it," the Irishman said. "But, lad, it's still a horse race."

Strain lined all their faces. Tension had seemingly charged and compressed the air; it was as if they were working under a bell, squeezed and cramped together, isolated from the world. There was a dry smell of dust, and steel shavings, and old documents around them, and another scent, acrid and sweet as jasmine, which told Peter that sweat was popping out all over Francois' body, coarsening the fragrance of his cologne.

Peter looked steadily at Bendell and the Irishman. "We're going to come through, lads. Trust me." He infused them with his own hard confidence, which was more glandular than realistic, for he believed they would come through, not because it was possible, but simply because they must.

The Irishman drew a deep breath, gripped the handle on the rim of the cutter-bar, and threw his weight against it. . . .

Peter went swiftly through the dark basement of the bank, following the slender beam of his flashlight. He checked his compass, followed a wall to its intersection with another, and then dropped to his knees beside a manhole cover that was secured by a screw lock with a ten-inch bar running through it. He spun the bar until the clamps came loose, raised the manhole lid and climbed down an iron ladder into the storm drains that twisted under the bank toward the river.

Something ran between his feet, claws ticking on slimy stones. Peter flicked his light about and the long slender beam leaped along the drain, flashing on drops of moisture beading the curving walls, brightening the dark rivulet of water running through the trough in the floor of the tunnel. The air was oppressively damp and cold, fetid with the smell of moss and sunless earth. In the springtime, he knew from what he read at the museum, the drains were deep with swiftly running water from the melting snows in the foothills of the Pyrenees. Now they were almost dry; the trickle in the bottom of the drain was hardly enough to dampen the old stones.

Peter followed the drain for perhaps a hundred yards, occasionally stopping to check his notes and compass. Within another fifty yards, the drain began to narrow; his head scraped against the rounded ceiling, and he went on at an awkward crouch, the beam of his torch describing an ever smaller arc between the compressing walls. At last he was forced to get on his knees and crawl, tucking the flashlight under his belt. After a dozen more yards the tunnel angled sharply right, and ran down to connect with another main drain. Light gleamed at the end of the tube which linked the two mains.

Peter flattened himself on his stomach and wormed his way down the connecting link for several yards, to make absolutely certain it was possible. He was wider in the shoulders than the Irishman and Francois, and he knew they could make it to the next main without any great difficulty.

The force of gravity was in his favor going down the slanting tube. But it worked against him when he tried to back out; pushing himself uphill turned out to be nearly impossible, for the confines of the link prevented him from getting a reliable leverage with his hands and feet. And there were cracks and ridges in the old stones which painfully scratched his knees and elbows, and impeded his progress, such as it was, by snagging his belt buckle, his flashlight, the buttons on his coat.

For a bleak moment he thought he might not make it. But he got out at last, and when he was free once more, his breath came harshly and raggedly, the sound grating against the damp walls. He had no love of stifling enclosures, and no affection at all for the creatures who had shared the tunnel with him, gaunt sewer rats whose claws made liquid, scratching noises on the slimy stones, and whose eyes were red and bold in the gloom beyond the range of his flashlight.

Peter backed out of the tunnel, stood when it widened, and ran along the drain to the ladder that led up to the basement of the bank. Time was now the destroyer; and the ticking of his watch seemed as fateful and ominous as the ticking of a bomb. . . .

The muscles in the Irishman's arms stood out rigidly. He was breathing hard, grunting as he turned the cutter-bar a fraction of an inch at a time, grinding fine diamond teeth deep into the steel of the vault. Bendell stood beside him, an appraising frown on his plump face.

"You should be close to the tumbler links."

"I should be in a pub on Grafton Street. How's the time, Peter?"

"Ten minutes."

"Good God!"

"Don't worry, we're on schedule," Peter said. "But listen: When the links break, you and Bendell will leave. I checked the route. It's clear. The second drain will take you out to the river a mile from town. Head for Biarritz and home, without wasting a second."

"And what about us?" Francois asked Peter.

"We stay and finish the job. We tie up the loose ends that can hang us."

"Very well." Francois shrugged, but there was a shine of sweat on his forehead, and the tic at the corner of his mouth was pulling rhythmically at his lips. . . .

At the front windows of the bank, Peter moved a shade with his fingertip, and looked into the street.

There was more traffic now: old women in dark shawls hurrying to Mass or to market; tourists taking pictures in the clear fresh sunlight; a stream of merrymakers with drums and goatskins of wine on their way to the Plaza del Castillo. The police detail stood at attention, waiting for the relief which would appear at the stroke of eight o'clock.

This fact had determined Peter's choice of time; in that split second of orderly commotion, when sergeants were barking commands, and tourists were taking pictures of the marching police, he had noticed a vacuum of security in which his plans would function with a minimal risk of detection.

He was preparing to let the shade fall back into place, when he saw a sight that made his mouth go dry.

The *Cabezuda* was coming along the street toward the bank, rocking from side to side, its staring eyes towering high above the heads of the crowd. Children laughed at it. Adults shouted good-humored insults at the huge, comically splayed nose, the flaming puffed-out cheeks.

"Good God!" Peter said softly, and looked at his watch.

They were three minutes early! What in hell had gone wrong? He cursed Angela, damning her piggishness, for that was the only explanation that occurred to him—that she couldn't wait a last precious minute to get her hands on the diamonds. Peter ran back to the vault. They would need a miracle now he knew, for the *Cabezuda* wouldn't be allowed to loiter in front of the bank.

The Irishman's face was a damp, straining mask, and under pale skin the muscles in his arms were bunched like knotted ropes.

"They're here," Peter said.

"We can't make it!"

Francois looked as if he had been struck a heavy blow at the base of the skull. He shook his head weakly. "No, no, they can't be here yet. It's not time."

Peter leaped to help the Irishman. Together they fought to turn the ring of diamond teeth against layered steel that had been forged to resist fires and explosions, to withstand anything but direct hits by bombs. Time became stretched and attentuated, until it seemed there was no time at all, but only the pain in their arms, the salty sweat in their eyes, the harsh noise of their breathing. And at last, there was an eternal interval, in which they hung their combined weight on the bar, hands slippery and weakening steadily, and it was then Peter realized that the great vault would not give way to their strength and prayers, that it had won and they had lost.

And at that instant there was a sudden crack deep inside the foot-thick layers of steel, and the chrome steel linkages grudgingly released their hold on bolts and tumblers.

220

The door swung open, and Francois was inside the vault with two long strides.

"Go now," Peter said to Bendell and the Irishman.

"Oh, God bless you, Peter," the Irishman said, sucking air deep into his lungs.

"Go, for the love of God. Go!"

They wrung his hands, scooped up their jackets, and raced through the gloom toward the stairs which led to the basement. Francois hurried from the vault with the Diamond Flutes of Carlos, and, in the dark light, it looked as if he were holding cylinders of frozen fire in his arms. Peter placed them on the length of chamois cloth and marvelled at their purity; there was something sacred in their flawless beauty, and he knew then —as he had known all along—that the price he must pay for this sacrilege would bankrupt his soul.

He placed the Net and Trident of Diamonds beside the Flutes of Carlos, and flipped the cloth about them, concealing their brilliance in a flexible tube of chamois that was about five inches thick and three feet long.

Then he looked sharply toward the front of the bank and saw the shadow of the *Cabezuda*, monstrous and huge, swaying across the green shades on the windows. There was still a chance, he realized, still a few seconds in which to pray for miracles. But as he ran through the bank, he had the strange conviction that they would make it. Yes, they would make it now. For unless they succeeded he would have no way to make amends. And he didn't believe for a minute that God would refuse him this last chance. It seemed to Peter as if he were doing everything from memory now, effortlessly and precisely.

He pulled the shade back, revealing the huge, rounded skull of the *Cabezuda* pressed against the iron grillwork, its bulk filling the window, blocking out all the light from the street. Peter tugged at the piece of tape, and a windowpane fell silently into his waiting hand. The aperture in the rear of the *Cabezuda* slid open. Peter lined it up with the empty window-frame, and fed the tube of chamois through the window, through the square of grillwork, and into the interior of the *Cabezuda*, where slim, white hands snaked it swiftly from sight.

It was over, finished, and Peter knew they had made it. Even before the glass and window shade were back in place, and the *Cabezuda* had lurched away from the side of the bank to sway into the street, even before these last swift links were connected, Peter knew everything was going to be all right.

"Get started now," he said to Francois, and moved the shade with his fingertip and looked into the street.

He heard the Frenchman's running footsteps going toward the stairs, and he saw, in the street below him, the *Cabezuda* swaying and listing precariously; but Peter knew it wouldn't fall, he knew there would be no ironical failure at this juncture—the broken shoestring, the chance malfunction of a traffic signal, the innocent parade of Girl Scouts blocking escape—no, nothing like that, no booby traps, no sneak punches now, they were home free, and all that remained was for Peter Churchman to pick up the check that would bankrupt him.

The police were steadying the *Cabezuda*. That was a delicious touch, he thought a bit sadly, a lovely grace note at the falling close of the song. Several of the policemen braced the swaying figure, steadied it, righted it, and, at last, sent it wandering along the streets with friendly slaps and shouts of encouragement.

And now it's all over, Peter thought with weary satisfaction. He stayed at the window until he saw the *Cabezuda* disappear around a corner. Then he walked through a marine translucence to the vault and began to put away the drills and punches. There was no point in tidying things up, of course, but, on the other hand, there was no reason not to.

And suddenly Peter froze. But the warning scream of his senses had come too late. He turned and tried to duck, but he was too late, far too late, to escape the blow that whistled softly through the air toward his head. The butt of a gun struck his left temple and knocked him sprawling to the floor.

A splinter of thought pierced the darkness in his mind. The film . . . but his strength was gone, his powers usurped by pain.

He heard only one thing more, the faint sound of

running footsteps. Soon they too were gone. . . .

The marble floor was cold against his cheek, and his limbs were filled with a shuddering impotence. And the darkness fell about him like the wings of a great black dove. . . .

 . . . . The *Cabezuda* lay on its side in the drafty shed by the river. The tip of its long, splayed nose rested on the dusty floor. Its broken eyes stared at the wall with a suggestion of lugubrious anger.

Phillip had demolished the huge head methodically. He had kicked holes through its eyes and forehead, smashed the drum that hung from its neck, ripped off the tricorn hat, and pulled the splintered wood apart with his hands.

The gaping interior of the *Cabezuda* was empty.

"Where are they?" he asked Angela.

Phillip held her by one arm, as he would a child, and looked into her eyes. Despite his exertions, his voice was gentle and reasonable, but it was the gentleness and reasonableness of a man who had a firm grip on the levers that operated a rack; there was no need to shout or scream, that was the victim's role. The look in his eyes sent a chill down Angela's spine.

"I told you the truth," she said. "Something went wrong. The window at the bank didn't open."

Phillip struck her across the face. "You can make this as difficult as you like. But I want the truth."

"Stop it, you pig!" She struggled fiercely against the

224

grip of his hand, but she might as well have tried to tear her arm from a vise.

Phillip struck her again, with more authority this time, and Angela's head snapped about on her shoulders like a flower in an erratic windstorm.

"Stop it!" she cried. "I told you the truth."

"Where is Francois?"

"I don't know. I don't know."

There was a sudden glimmer of understanding in Phillip's eyes. "I should have kept in mind that swine's talent for betrayal. You must have given him the diamonds on the way from the bank. While I was carting you through the streets and alleys."

"I swear to God I didn't. Oh listen to me, you great stupid pig! Peter's tricked us. Don't you realize that?"

"No, you and Francois are the specialists in that area. So let's see which you prefer: the diamonds or your pretty face."

"No, stop it!"

After a while Phillip was forced to consider the possibility that she might be telling the truth. He released her arm, frowned at his watch, and went swiftly through the door, without another glance at Angela, who lay huddled on the dusty floor beside the smashed head of the *Cabezuda*.

A scream waked Peter. Or so it seemed, as he rolled onto his side and sat up, bracing his weight with a hand against the floor. The silence in the dim interior of the bank was troubled by echoes; it was like the trembling silence in a room in which a telephone has just stopped ringing.

The lump above his ear pulled his right eye into a squint. His head ached dreadfully. He got to his knees and looked through the tool kit, driven to this by the kind of pointless hope that impels a starving dog to return with futile persistence to an empty plate.

But of course it was gone; the can of film was gone. Dear sweet Christ, he thought wearily. That was why Francois hadn't bothered to kill him. He hadn't needed to. Peter got to his feet, and breathed slowly and deeply, summoning the last of his strength for what lay ahead of him.

He had been prepared to pick up the check, to make amends, to pay the bill with his freedom. But he couldn't do that now. For when Angela sent the film to the police, the prison doors would swing shut on Bendell and the Irishman too.

It was ten-thirty. Francois had a long start on him. But there was still Phillip, the one last hope, the one threat Francois could have no way of anticipating. . . .

. . . . Peter lowered himself through the manhole, climbed down into the big drain which ran under the basement of the bank. The cold and dampness now seemed more intense; he could see his breath in the gleam of his flashlight, hazy and white on the heavy, fetid air.

He ran along the tunnel until it began to narrow; then he went to his knees to cover the last half-dozen yards. He was quite weak, but his mind was functioning clearly. Nothing very subtle or complex had occurred to him however; find Francois and recover the can of film, those were his simple goals.

And for all practical purposes, Peter achieved both these ends by the unspectacular and unheroic act of pointing the beam of his flashlight down the narrow link between the two mains.

What he saw nearly made him retch. He snapped off the light, but there were still hotly glowing little eyes, and the scratch of claws on slimy stones, to remind him of what horrors had been revealed in the glare of his torch.

Francois had had a long start on him, to be sure, but this was as far as he had got; his body was lodged in the narrow connecting tube, and there it would stay until the fall floods swept it into the next main, and then on to the river.

Peter drew a deep breath and snapped on his light. He forced himself to look down the tube, and then he saw and understood what had happened to Francois: The can of film, tucked under his belt, had become wedged into a crack in the stone surfacing of the tube. One of its flanged rims had been driven deeply into the fissure, and Francois, with his arms thrust ahead of his body, and his weight pressing heavily on the can of film, had been unable to free himself; the confines of the tube had made it impossible for him to shift his weight or move his arms.

With his body slanting downward at a forty-five degree angle, the Frenchman's cramped hands and feet had been totally impotent against the force of gravity. He couldn't slide down to the big main ahead of him; and he couldn't fight his way back up and out of the connecting tube.

All he could do was scream.

And that hadn't deterred the rats for long. . . .

Peter followed the light of his torch back along the tunnel, and up to the basement of the bank. His capacity for irony was sufficient to allow him to appreciate, if not to relish, the appropriateness of Francois' fate. But he couldn't manage a philosophical shrug at the punch line of this bitter joke. For now he was trapped just as helplessly as the Frenchman had been.

Francois' betrayal had worked out quite neatly, although not in the manner he had intended it to. He had planned to destroy Peter Churchman, and he had managed it by blocking the only route to freedom with his dead body.

There was still the other exit, the shaft they had blasted from the basement of the adjoining warehouse. But this offered little hope now. It was eleven in the morning, and the plaza and sidewalks in front of the passageway would be clogged with traffic and pedestrians. But Peter made a reconnaissance anyway, crawling through the shaft and peering cautiously from the window into the passageway. His estimate of conditions had been conservative, he saw: Not only were there crowds surging by, but at the juncture of the passageway and the street stood a broad-shouldered policeman, his back to Peter, his eyes flicking alertly over the people and traffic passing before him. He was fifteen feet from Peter, and despite the fact that he rocked slowly from side to side on his stout boots, he gave the impression of being as rooted to the spot as a tree in the ground.

Peter waited hopefully for him to leave. If the policeman went away, he might try to open the window, remove the grillwork, and climb into the passageway, taking the long, long chance that no one would notice him crawling out of the basement in broad daylight.

But after fifteen minutes he decided it was no use. Peter returned to the second floor of the bank, and sat wearily at a desk near the open vault. Don't quit, he thought. As long as you can think, there's a chance. But he found he didn't really believe this. He felt he had never been a player in this game, but only a pawn. And so what was there to think about? He opened drawers and looked at paperclips and rubber bands and pencils. At ledgers, notebooks, files. He drummed his fingers on the desk, drowning at inkwells, calendars, a telephone, a spike fluttering with flimsy papers.

Suddenly he sat up straighter. He rubbed his hands together nervously and picked up the phone. In his ear the operator's voice sounded, small and crisp: *"Digame?"*

Peter let out his breath and replaced the receiver in its cradle. He had an electrical link to the outside world— But how could he use it?

He stood and paced in front of the desk, frowning at the phone. In his career, he realized, he had departed the scenes of crimes by a variety of means: fast cars, airplanes, a tractor on one occasion, a helicopter on another, and—in Venice, this was—by speedboat.

But he had never had an occasion to use the most conventional method of all, and he wondered if this were the time to chalk up a first. He decided it had to be. Peter said a hasty prayer, which he realized he could expect no results from, and picked up the telephone. When the operator answered, he said: "If you please, I'd like to order a taxi. Yes . . . now let me tell you where I'll be standing. . . ."

The cab driver was a plump, middle-aged philosopher who relished arguments with Authority, not because he believed he might ever win one, but because he believed he served a useful function in keeping Authority awake and on its toes. What he feared was a drowsy Authority, for he believed that the somnolent exercise of power created excesses; orders given with yawns, surveillance through sleepy eyes, and the like.

And so, for the third time, he said to the policeman: "My dispatcher directed me here. I don't drive about whimsically."

Horns sounded behind him. He had stopped at the intersection of the passageway and the street.

The policeman, whose name was Carlos, blew his whistle and waved an arm. "You're blocking traffic. Drive on."

"Permit me to make one point. Think of the client who ordered this taxi. Think of my dispatcher. And think of me, please. I am not a free agent. I am an instrument serving the orderly—"

"Drive on! Drive on!"

"—needs of transport in our city."

Carlos blew his whistle. The stalled traffic raised a clamor that soared in dizzying blasts above the plaza.

"A last point, if you please."

"No! No!"

"Very well, I have tried."

Peter tapped Carlos on the shoulder. "Excuse me, please."

Carlos turned and blinked at him. "Yes, of course."

Peter climbed into the cab and gave the driver the name of his hotel.

"One moment," Carlos said.

"Yes?"

231

Carlos frowned uncertainly at Peter. "Senor Churchman?"

"Why, yes."

"We've met before, I think."

"Oh yes, so we did."

Horns honked. The driver sighed. "May I proceed?"

"No. One moment." Carlos scratched his ear and looked down the passageway, studying its blank walls and barred windows. Senor Churchman had emerged from this passageway, which was quite literally impossible. As Carlos pondered the puzzle, his fingers trembled for a pencil and notebook, and the official phrases to describe the incident began to march in orderly sequence through his mind. But then he recalled that Senor Churchman had earned the right to wear the Order of the Blue Star. And he recalled too, with a pang of self-pity, the icy smile of the superior who had lectured him with such exquisite sarcasm on the distinction between the calls of duty and the calls of nature.

Carlos sighed and waved the cab on.

13 ❧

THE WATERING TRUCKS had gone and the breezes in the Plaza del Castillo were fragrant with the clean smell of damp earth and flowers. Lights from the cafés bordering the square gleamed softly on the wet pavements and sidewalks. In the gutters the frothing water was crested with cigarette stubs and artificial flowers and torn bullfight tickets. And down all the drains in steady streams sailed business cards and matchbook covers with addresses and telephone numbers scribbled on them.

Waiters stood at ease in the terraces of the cafes, cheerfully attentive to half-filled tables. No fire-bulls exploded in the streets, no rockets or drums shook the air, and no lines of dancers twisted through the plaza —for the week of San Fermin had come to an end.

It was a bittersweet moment, a time to forget passion

233

and excitement, a time to return to the matters of a practical world, but passion could not be forgotten so easily, so quickly, and a residue of it seemed to tremble on the quiet air, like the melody of a half-remembered song; but in those faint echoes, fainter with each passing moment, was the promise of the eventual silence, the inevitable loss, that would tend the wake of the death of passion.

"Peter, you must keep one simple fact in mind, and you must cheer up," Morgan said.

"And what is that simple fact?"

"Well, let me see." Morgan frowned and stroked his lush blond beard. "It's quite easy to give way to doubt and confusion. It's a question of getting off the tracks." He tapped his forehead significantly. "Up here. I'm beginning to have an uneasy feeling about heretics, Peter."

Peter was silent. He had no heart for talk; his world lay in pieces at his feet, and he was certain that no one —least of all himself—could ever make it whole again.

"Well, that's one way of looking at it, I suppose," Morgan said. "Heretics, you see, allow the engine of faith to—leap, that's it, leap off the tracks of conviction—" He looked at the sky, frowning. "Yes. To leap off the tracks of conviction—and, yes, plunge, that's it, *plunge* into the gorges of error."

"As it were," Peter said wearily.

"Yes. As it were. So don't let that happen to you,

Peter. Just remember this one simple fact: She did it all for you. Everything Grace did was for your sake."

"I once had an enormous talent for self-delusion. I'm praying it hasn't deserted me. Because I want to believe you."

They sat at a table on the terrace of the Café Kutz looking out across the dark expanse of the Plaza del Castillo.

"But you must, Peter. You must. Don't get off the track. She knew Angela didn't intend to play fair. Those were her exact words. Grace has very strict notions about fair play, you see."

"Against all the evidence to the contrary, I'm trying to believe that too."

But no matter how hard he tried, Peter could not believe; he could not even pretend to believe; and there was no logic yet devised or conceived that could brace his spinning thoughts.

For it had not been Angela who had arrived three minutes early at the bank; it had been Grace!

"Fair play means everything to her," Morgan said, nodding judiciously. "That's why she ordered the *Cabezuda* made. That's why she made me carry it to the bank. Before Angela got there."

Peter shook his head helplessly. He couldn't speak.

"I'm quite strong, you know," Morgan said with a sigh. "It caused a great deal of trouble in schools. Because I had an aversion to things. They used to get at

235

me." He smiled gently; happy lights sparkled in his eyes. "Then I had to break them up. I broke up the boiler in a school once. It kept making popping noises at me. But that's all over. It's people now. Lawyers, heretics, that sort of thing. So cheer up. She did it all for you, Peter."

The majestic ingenuity of her betrayal, had left Peter without a reed of hope to cling to.

"Then where is she?"

"Well, I don't know."

"Where are the diamonds?"

Morgan frowned and tapped his forehead. "She was a deep one. Do you remember Quince?"

"No."

"Grace rather puts me in mind of old Quince. Deep sorts. Afraid of things causing rows. You would have liked Quince. He lives in Wales. Do you think we could find him?"

"I don't know, and I don't give a damn."

"That doesn't sound like you, Peter. I thought you might want to look up Quince."

"I want Grace. I want to know, once and for all, how great and blind a fool I've been."

Had it all been a charade? Had she been using him from the very start? Was nothing true and real? And where in the name of God was she now? Seated in the first-class cabin of a jet thundering toward Melbourne or Lima? Warming the stewardess with a radiant smile? While one slim hand rested lightly on a valise filled with diamonds?

Peter knew that he, too, must now start thinking in terms of jet airplanes and distant places. For in the morning, ten hours from now, the doors of the Banco de Bilbao would be opened, and, within minutes, rockets would go screaming up from every police bureau in Europe. The chase would be on!

Angela and Phillip had long since gone their separate ways. She had accepted Francois' death realistically. And so had Phillip, although the nature of that death had caused him to muse with grim satisfaction on the infinite complexity of God's justice.

Peter had talked to Angela before she left Pamplona. She had been bitter but philosophical about the loss of the diamonds, and the loss of her hold on him; but Peter knew her far too well to be reassured by this seemingly stoic acceptance of defeat. Inside she was roiling. He had sensed there was only one thing Angela couldn't abide—that he might escape the destruction she and Francois had planned for him.

The sword of her vengeance hung over him by a single, silken thread, but he didn't have the heart to care one way or the other; he longed for only two things, which now seemed hopelessly incompatible—Grace and truth.

"Please tell me everything one more time," he said to Morgan.

"Yes, but remember to stay on the track. Don't go plunging off. Well then. She knew Angela wouldn't play fair. I've mentioned that, I think. So she ordered a *Cabezuda* from the same chap who made yours. A twin, so to speak. Now then. Do you remember the log-chopping contests? Well, she arranged for one of those Basques to carry the *Cabezuda*."

Dear God, Peter thought, more black mystery. "You didn't tell me that before," he said.

"Didn't I?" Morgan frowned faintly. "Odd. Well, in any case, she decided to let me help. Fair play again, you see. I'd mistaken you for a lawyer, and caused all sorts of trouble, so she gave me a chance to make it all right again."

Peter sighed. "Did she happen to mention airplane schedules? Or whether she might need a parka where she was going? Or just a bikini and sun lotion?"

"No, but there is one other thing. She said this would be a bit of a shock to you. She asked me to explain it very gently. Fair play again, you'll notice."

Peter sighed again. "Well, the sentiment does her credit, I guess."

A stout, uniformed figure came hurrying across the plaza. Antonio, the policeman, mounted the steps of the terrace, his short legs churning with a sense of urgency. He sank breathlessly into a chair at Peter's table, removed his hat and fanned his flushed face.

"Antonio! Are you all right?"

"Yes. No."

"What's the matter?"

Antonio tried to smile, but the effort only emphasized the anxiety in his eyes. He drew a deep breath and said: "Peter, this is probably a joke. Maybe we can have a good laugh about it later." He took an envelope from the inner breast pocket of his tunic, and Peter sighed faintly as he recognized the writing on it. Antonio removed several sheets of folded stationery from the envelope, shook them open with fluttering fingers.

"Of course, I know this is all nonsense," he said, smiling nervously at Peter. "Sheer nonsense. Forgive me for seeming to take it so seriously, but I must have your assurance—" He stopped and drew another deep breath. "This note was left at my hotel several hours ago. I just received it. There is no signature, of course. People who make such reckless charges seldom have the courage to sign their names to them. But we must discuss it, Peter. Purely as a matter of routine. You understand, of course."

"Of course," Peter said, and waited for Angela's sword to fall.

Antonio put on his glasses and studied the sheets of paper. Then he shrugged. "This is ridiculous. It says that you bought blasting equipment at the Terremoto Construction Company in Malaga last week. Which would be a simple matter to check. It also says that you acquired certain tools and equipment from Mr. Shahari in Gibraltar, and smuggled them into Spain. With the help of a tinker, whose name isn't given. A convenient oversight. Well, here's the last of it. Whoever wrote this irresponsible drivel claims you blasted open the vault of the Banco de Bilbao this morning." Antonio laughed. "Yes. That's what it says. And that you stole the Flutes of Carlos. And the Net and Trident which adorned the Virgin of Seville. I'm embarrassed to repeat such absurdities. But I must, Peter. For only one reason: to hear your denial."

Peter stared at the back of his hands.

Antonio's smile became uncertain; then it faded slowly from his lips. After a moment, he said: "Now I must ask you a question, Peter."

"Yes, I understand."

"Is any of this true?"

"It's all true, I regret to say."

Antonio looked away and blinked his eyes. "I am a policeman, but I find that I don't care whether it's true or not. Strange, eh?"

"We were friends."

"We are friends." Antonio blew his nose. "I can't judge you. But you realize what I must do, Peter. I must ask you to come with me to the Administration of Police."

"I understand."

The policeman's eyes were sad. "We can walk across the square like old friends taking a stroll after dinner.

Chatting about something that happened when we were young. Something amusing, eh?"

"Yes. Do you remember the time when the burro got drunk in my bar?"

"Yes, yes. That was very funny. He butted the priest, didn't he?"

"That's right."

"Are you ready then?"

Peter nodded and climbed slowly to his feet.

"It's only a short walk," Antonio said.

A distant drumbeat sounded on the air, and a single flute drew a lovely looping line through the clear mild night. At the opposite end of the plaza there were strange flashes of light, and faint cheers that rose toward the sky like jubilant prayers.

Antonio put a hand on Peter's arm. "Shall we go?"

A lighter hand touched Peter's other arm. "Oh, darling, I'm so terribly sorry," Grace said.

Peter closed his eyes. He knew this was an hallucination, a sensory malfunction engineered by his subconscious. But it gave him the strength he needed. In his mind there was a vision of Grace at his side, her head golden against the night, her eyes luminous with tenderness and love. And in this curious trance, he believed a lie, believed that everything had worked itself out serenely; they had nothing to fear any more, nothing to do but love one another for the rest of their lives. And Peter realized that as long as he kept his eyes shut, he was safe from harm; as long as her dear face blazed radiantly in his thoughts, he was free for all time, intact and invulnerable.

The cheering was louder now, but the drum and bugle soared triumphantly above it. There was a stir in the great square.

"Darling, please look at me."

Peter opened his eyes. Grace stood beside him, her head golden against the night, a tender, anxious smile on her lips.

"Where the hell have you been?" he said sharply.

She raised her voice to make herself heard above the cheering. "Please don't be angry."

"Why did you run out on me? And why in God's name did you come back? We're finished. Angela's blown the whistle!"

"Please, my darling, I hated worrying you. But I had to do it this way. When the guards were gone for dinner. When she was all alone. It was our only chance."

"What the devil are you talking about?"

"Look. There."

Peter turned and blinked his eyes. "Good God," he said shakily.

From the balconies ringing the square, floodlights crisscrossed in blindingly brilliant patterns. On the terraces of the cafés, people stood clapping and cheering.

The small statue of the Virgin of Santa Maria was making a last triumphant tour of the Plaza del Castillo.

She swayed rhythmically with the lurching strides of the smiling men who supported the float, her blank, girlish eyes shining in the glare of the floodlights.

In her slender rigid arms glistened the Trident of Diamonds. The golden mesh of the Net of Diamonds was pinned to her smooth plaster brow like a wedding veil. And at her feet blazed the diamond Flutes of Carlos. The wildflowers scattered about the float, the poppies and daisies, the fragile blue iris, glowed softly in the radiant reflections of the gems.

Antonio moved like a sleepwalker to the edge of the terrace, his mouth hanging open, his eyes going blankly from the figure of the Virgin to the sheets of writing paper in his hand.

"It was our only chance," Grace said quietly.

"It won't work, darling."

"It must. You wanted to give yourself up. I knew that. But you can't."

Peter blinked again, for he had noticed something else about the Virgin; a diamond tiara sparkled on her head; a lovely little crown he had last seen shining like a corona above Grace's golden hair.

"Why did you give it to her?"

"I don't know. It was a way of getting at my soul, I think. With a pail and brush. It's so strange, Peter. It may have worked. I feel wonderful. It's like a miracle."

"Oh quite," Morgan said, heaving himself to his feet and nodding approvingly at the approaching figure of the Virgin. "A miracle, no doubt of it."

The word trembled on the air. A priest standing nearby crossed himself, far from casually. Waiters exchanged glances.

"Yes, yes," Antonio said, but he seemed quite agitated as he looked at Peter. "Did you do this because—" He stopped and started over again. "Peter, did you take my cynical attitude seriously? Did you think our poor little Santa Maria would be humbled and slighted because—" He shook his head helplessly. "What I'm trying to say is this: Did you steal these things, borrow them, that is, so that our Virgin might enjoy this one moment of glory?"

Morgan smiled ominously at him. "Don't get off the track. Don't let the engine of faith plunge—" He frowned at Peter. "Where did it plunge?"

"Into the gorge of error."

"Quite. Keep that in mind," Morgan said. "It's a miracle, no question about it. I should hate to meet a heretic in Spain, of all places."

"I share your view. Naturally." Antonio blew out his cheeks. "Why should I be stubborn? I have the option of believing my friend is a thief, or believing in the power of Almighty God to work miracles. Why should I refuse to believe what's before my eyes?"

They were all insane, Peter thought sadly. For this would never work. . . .

The waiters had passed out rolls of streamers, and

opened fresh boxes of confetti. And soon these were sparkling and flashing through the air, twisting about the figure of the Virgin, falling in serpentine loops on the carpet of wild flowers at her feet.

"We must contribute in our own fashion," Antonio said, and ripped Angela's letter into three, roughly equal sections. He gave one to Grace, another to Peter, and kept a section for himself. This he proceeded to tear into bits. At last he had a handful of paper scraps, decorated gaily but improbably with meaningless fragments of Angela's handwriting.

He cheered and threw them into the air.

"How pretty!" Grace delicately ripped her section of the letter into pieces, and let the wind sweep them off the palm of her hand.

Insane, Peter thought wearily. Insane.

"What are you waiting for, darling?"

Peter looked at Antonio. "There are still some practical considerations," he said.

"Yes?"

"The open vault in the bank, for instance."

Antonio shrugged. "They will blame it on the good thief, Saint Dismus. Or *a* good thief. It hardly matters. Peter, nothing has been stolen."

"But listen to me. Don't you realize that—"

Antonio interrupted him. "Peter, the north of Spain wanted a bit of our southern mystery and romance to mingle with their excellent hotels and practical plumbing. Well, we have obliged them. How they adjust to it is no concern of ours."

St. Dismus, the good thief, Peter thought, and smiled as he remembered the last line of an old poem, "—a thief to the end, who, with his last breath, stole Paradise."

He had spoken aloud, and Morgan nodded, and said: "As it were."

Peter tore the last of Angela's letter into bits, and let them drop to the ground at his feet. Then he put an arm around Grace, and they walked into the plaza with Morgan and Antonio, to join the crowd following the sparkling figure of the Virgin into the night.

Grace put her cheek against his arm, and smiled up at him, and Peter knew that he had come through once again, but finally and forever this time.

"Darling, the tiara isn't really valuable. The diamonds are paste. Do you suppose that matters?"

"Well, no. The gesture is what counts, I should think."

"Oh, Peter, you're such a solid man."

He held her closer and they went smiling through the beams of the floodlights, under a sky that was as soft and dark as the wings of a black dove.